SUE FOR MERCY

SUE FOR MERCY

Veronica Heley

CHIVERS

British Library Cataloguing in Publication Data available

This Large Print edition published by BBC Audiobooks Ltd, Bath, 2008.
Published by arrangement with the Author.

U.K. Hardcover ISBN 978 I 405 64570 6
U.K. Softcover   ISBN 978 I 405 64571 3

Printed and bound in Great Britain by
Antony Rowe Ltd., Chippenham, Wiltshire

ONE

It wasn't safe to go on driving. I was crying so hard I could hardly see the road through the sleet of the January storm. I turned off the main road, looking for a quiet place in which to park while I blew my nose and cleaned my glasses. I told myself that I was tired, that it was late, and that it wasn't my fault that I was short-sighted and had to wear glasses. Even if I was a trifle overweight, there had been no need for that horrible man at the party to make jokes at my expense. One day I would meet someone who didn't mind that my bust was slightly too big for current fashions; my skin was clear and my eyes a reasonable size. 'That Cow!' the man had said.

A sports car came up behind me, its headlights dazzling my already blurred eyesight. I slowed, refusing to panic. We were travelling along a winding, sparsely-lit road of detached houses. The driver of the sports car leant on his horn, which was not only bad manners, but also illegal after midnight. He closed up on me, which showed poor road sense on a winding road. No doubt he and his passenger were swearing at me for being an over-cautious woman driver. A second car came up behind the first, also with its headlights full on. It lit up the interior of the sports car, throwing the figures of the driver and passenger into silhouette.

I signalled, slowed and turned left into someone's private driveway so as to allow them to pass. At the same time I hoped, uncharitably, that one or other of the road hogs might come to grief on the sharp bend in the road which lay just ahead.

By the time I had blown my nose, cleaned my glasses and resumed my journey, the road ahead ought to have been dark, but it wasn't. I could see the lights of the cars even before I rounded the corner, and I guessed what I should see even though I hadn't heard the crash. Sure enough, the sports car had mounted the opposite pavement and come to rest with one wing crumpled against someone's garden wall. The lights were on inside the car, and from the driver's seat, a rag doll of a body spilled head down on to the wet pavement. The second car had pulled up some twenty-five yards further on, and at first I thought the situation was under control—until I realised that the man and the woman were running away from, and not towards the scene of the accident. Even as I watched, they climbed into the back of the second car and it drove away, rear lights winking.

I braked, slushily. Sleet drummed against the wind-screen. I was used to dealing with emergencies, being in charge of the typing pool at Murchison's Chemical Works, a

2

position usually held by a much older woman, but I wasn't used to dealing with dead bodies, and I assumed that the victim of the car accident was dead, or the people from the second car wouldn't have left him lying there, half in and half out of his car. And what about the woman who had been his passenger? She must have abandoned him, too. Cowards! I thought. They might at least have pushed him back into the car out of the rain, and surely one of them could have stayed with him while the others went for help. Then something about the body caught my attention; dead men don't bleed, and the young man's hand was turning from white to dark red as I looked at it.

I fished out my headscarf and tied it on, buttoning my raincoat high before stepping out into the storm. The car which had crashed was a dark blue, almost new MGB. It had been well cared for, and recently cleaned. It looked as if the wing was only slightly dented, but the driver must have tried to jump clear at the moment of im-pact to explain his injuries. If he'd stayed put, he'd probably have got away with a bumped forehead, and if he'd been wearing his seat belt, he'd not have been hurt at all.

As it was . . .

Drunk! I thought.

He was wearing a white shirt, unbuttoned at the neck, no tie, grey slacks, black shoes and socks. His eyes were closed and there was blood on his bright hair. Blood was also trickling down from one corner of his mouth. His legs were twisted; maybe he'd caught a foot under a pedal in his leap for safety. He looked about twenty-five years old and was exceedingly handsome.

I could feel his heart beat draggingly against my fingers through the soaked rag of his shirt. His hair was losing its brightness and beginning to curl in tendrils close to his head. The handkerchief which had been wound round his left hand fell away as I tried to lift him back into the car, revealing fingers covered with blood. Also, his thumb looked out of joint. I sniffed and recoiled, for he stank of whisky.

Sleet chilled my face and legs. I hesitated. The fool deserved all he got, driving round these badly-lit roads in an inconsiderate manner, drunk . . .

Stop—hold everything! This wasn't the man who had been driving the sports car. In my mind's eye I could recall the silhouettes of the man and woman who had been in the sports car as it drove up behind me. The driver had been wearing a hat and had an overcoat or scarf high up round his ears. I rather thought he had been wearing glasses. His passenger had not been wearing a hat, but she had been wearing some dark coat or jacket, and had a scarf tied over her hair. I checked the injured

4

man and his car; no jacket, no overcoat, no glasses. And there was a trace of fresh blood on the back seat.

Once more I tried to lift him back into the car, but he was a big-boned man, and although I was no midget, I didn't succeed. I could, however, pull him out into the road so that he lay in a more comfortable position, and this I did. All the time I was trying to remember what it was that had struck me as odd about the second car. I thought it was probably a 1300, with a yellow number plate. Newish. Then I got it; the man and the woman I had seen running away from the crash were the people I had previously seen as driver and passenger of the sports car. I had seen the woman quite clearly as she ducked into the waiting car. She had been wearing a dark trouser suit and her headscarf was a brilliant red. Both the man and the woman had got into the back seats of the second car, which had shot off immediately. This meant that there must be at least one, and possibly two more people who knew of the accident and had decided to do nothing about it. It was getting complicated.

In the meantime, the injured man was getting wet, and needed medical attention. Not a single car had passed.

I dithered. Should I leave him and go for help? It seemed I must do so. I started to run down the road towards the nearest drive, thinking how very unfair life was. There was I, condemned to wear glasses, despairingly conscious that I was not pretty, and there was this young man as handsome as the day was long, who had probably got perfect sight and perfect teeth, and a dozen girl-friends, and didn't care for any of them. The first house I came to was in darkness, and I couldn't get anyone to come to the door; of course it was well after midnight by that time, and I didn't really blame them, but . . .

I ran back down the drive and almost under the wheels of a car being driven slowly along the middle of the road. It was an ancient family car, containing a middle-aged man and his wife with two fretful little girls. They had been away for the weekend, and broken down on the motorway on their way back. The driver was kind enough to help me load the injured man into the back of my Mini before going on his way. By that time I was as wet as my passenger.

The drive to the hospital was a nightmare. Several times I thought the injured man had stopped breathing.

A nurse took one look at him and ordered up a stretcher, a doctor and a trolley full of instruments. I hovered, uncertain whether to stay or go. It was nearly one o'clock, and I was worn out. When the nurse came out of the cubicle into which she had taken my passenger, I asked how he was, and whether I could go. She said I'd better ask the doctor, who wanted to have a word with me, anyway. So I waited, wet and uncomfortable. I found a radiator, and leaned against it, steaming.

'This man!' said a voice. I snapped to attention. I must have dozed off. The man I had picked off the pavement was being wheeled past me into the interior of the hospital, his eyes still closed, looking as classically handsome as before. 'What's his name?' asked the doctor.

I told him what I knew, which wasn't much. It didn't satisfy me as a story, and it didn't satisfy the doctor, either. I wound up by saying I supposed the injured man had been at a party which had got a bit rough, and had been dumped in the street after the car crash, as a joke.

'I don't think so,' said the doctor. 'Broken collar-bone, a dislocated thumb, slashed fingers, extensive bruising to thighs, possible fracture of the skull . . . that's what I've found so far, and I've hardly begun. You say you smelled whisky on him? But that he definitely wasn't driving?'

'No, he wasn't driving, I'm sure of that.'

We looked each other in the eye. He said the matter would have to be reported to the police, and took my name and address. I could see he didn't think such in-juries had been caused by a frolic at a party, or by a car crash. It left a nasty taste in my mouth as I went home to bed.

*   *   *

I don't suppose I'd have taken the matter any further if Bessie hadn't interfered. She was secretary to the Managing Director at work, and also my best friend. She was a fuzzy-headed blonde whose fashionable image overlaid exceptional secretarial skills and lots of common sense. She was keeping the Assistant Production Manager on a string until he promised to give up smoking, and had already picked out the ring and the house which she wanted him to buy.

Bessie and I spent much of our free time together. She thought I under-rated myself, urged me to diet, and took me to parties with her. She knew all about my abortive romance with Rob, one of the housemen at the hospital, which had cost me my virginity and my confidence a couple of years back, and although she quite approved of my leaving home to live in a flat by myself afterwards, she did not approve of my spending more money on my new home than on my wardrobe. She would tell me that if I only stopped being self-conscious about my appearance, I would find plenty of men anxious to go out with me. She said I was prickly, and self-centred, and that if I could only remember that others might be as shy as I, all my social problems would be solved. When Bessie said these things, I listened, and told her I wished very much that I could follow her advice, as I was sure that she was right.

'Sue Stephens, you're only twenty-five,' she would wail. 'You act as if you were forty-five!'

'I feel it sometimes,' I would say, and help myself to another Chelsea Bun. I always turned to food when I was feeling miserable, as I did on the day following that disastrous party.

'Well, how did it go?' asked Bessie, who had fixed the invitation for me.

'All right,' I said cautiously, helping myself to a double ration of chips. 'But they served both wine and beer, and the mixture gave me a headache.' Then before she could show her exasperation, I told her what had happened on the way home, concluding, 'So I left him at the hospital, looking just as beautiful as that chap in Ben Hur—almost Grecian, or do I mean Roman? All laid out under a clean sheet.'

'He might have died of exposure if you hadn't come along.'

'Possible fracture of the skull . . . what a pity. I hope they didn't have to cut his hair away it's sort of blond with a bit of ginger in it, longish and brushed back, but trying to curl.' I helped myself to treacle tart and custard.

'Has he snuffed it yet?'

'How should I know?'

'Ring up, poppet. He's your find, isn't he? You acted the Good Samaritan, and you're entitled to know how your man's getting on.'

She swept me back to the empty office and stood over me while I dialled. I giggled a little, feeling daring. I tracked my quarry down to the Men's General Ward. The Sister's voice on the other end of the line was distant and tinny.

'Mr. Ashton, you mean? As comfortable as can be expected, what with concussion and his hand . . . This is Mrs. Ashton speaking?'

'No, I just found him and brought him to the hospital.'

'I'm afraid we're not allowed to give information to anybody but his family. Visiting hours are from seven to eight. Prompt.' She was a busy woman, and I was wasting her time.

'Oh—well, if I could phone his family, perhaps?'

'I have no idea where they might be. He says they are away. They certainly haven't been enquiring for him.'

'What—no one? No one's been to see him?'

'His employer phoned, and his landlady, but no one has been to see him. Seven to eight sharp, mind.' She put the phone down.

I relayed the information to Bessie, adding that the Sister had seemed to think I would visit him, since no one else had. Bessie seemed to take it for granted that I would, too.

'He's your very own patient, isn't he? But for you, he'd be dead. At least give him the opportunity to thank you for saving his life.'

'Don't exaggerate! But I could drop in for five minutes on the way to evening classes, I suppose.'

I had to admit to some curiosity. I took along a box of After Eight mints. If I didn't think it necessary to give them to him, I could always eat them myself.

'Mr. Ashton?' repeated a nurse in mid-flight. 'Far end on the left.'

He was staring up at the ceiling, not expecting visitors. His hair had been brushed back and away from his forehead; bright and halo-like against the white of the hospital pillow, almost like a Burne-Jones saint. His face was greenish-white, there were heavy shadows under his eyes and the deep line of a frown divided eyebrows which were many shades darker than his hair. His left arm lay across his chest, the hand heavily bandaged. He looked barely conscious and as if he had a cracking headache. I was standing over him before he realised anyone had come to see him, and his eyes focused on me slowly and with difficulty.

'I'm Sue Stephens,' I said, helpfully. 'I found you after the car crash, and brought you here.'

His eyes were the true light grey not often seen without some adulteration of green or

11

brown flecks. His brows were levelled with pain.

'Sue!' he repeated. I thought I could detect pleasure in his voice. 'That's nice,' he said, and I felt myself relax into a smile. I sat down and put the box of chocolates on the bed near his right hand.

'Do you like them?' I asked. 'Because if not . . .'

He moved his head, and then wished he hadn't, judging by the way his eyelids contracted against pain.

'Shall I fetch someone for you?' I asked, looking round for a nurse. The ward was filling up with visitors carrying sheaves of chrysanthemums and potted plants, women with heavy overcoats muffling their shapes, carrying shopping baskets filled with goodies for their menfolk. Mr. Ashton's locker was bare except for a huge basket of fruit; a professionally arranged job. I tried to see if I could read the card with it, but it was turned away from me.

'No—better in a moment' he said. 'I don't like dope, anyway. Makes it difficult to concentrate.' He moved his head again, this time to see my face. Helpfully I pulled my chair forward, closer to the bed. 'You found me?'

'Half in and half out of the car, soaking wet and reeking of whisky.' I couldn't help sounding censorious; I didn't admire people who lost self-control enough to get drunk. Mind you, this lad didn't look a weakling. It had probably been a rare event with him.

'Drunk, was I?' He seemed to have some difficulty in taking in the sense of what I had said.

'Very drunk. Don't you remember?'

'Nothing. I remember locking up on Friday night at Whitestones, and I think I can remember driving away, but . . .' His eyes flickered and drooped.

'It was late on Monday night that I found you. No, after midnight on Monday, so it was really Tuesday morning. This is Tuesday now, you know.'

'So they tell me,' he said, still dreamily. 'It's a side effect of concussion, apparently. Sometimes you don't remember what happened just before you got hit on the head. Sometimes you forget just a few minutes, sometimes a few hours. They say the memory usually returns after a while. I seem to have forgotten three days. Tell me, though is the car badly damaged?'

'The MGB is yours? One wing crumpled against a wall. It's not bad. I suppose the police will have towed it away and you'll have to ask them to let you have it back.'

His mouth and eyes contracted. 'Drunk in charge. Of course.'

'But you weren't . . .'

'Technically, I was.'

13

He'd slipped up, there. If he knew he hadn't been driving, then he wasn't suffering from amnesia, and he did know what he'd been doing since last Friday night. I hesitated, and then decided he wasn't well enough for me to press the matter.

His eyelids were shut. I sat back in my chair and looked around. There was a pleasant hum of voices in the ward, men and women chatting and arguing and ribbing each other. A huge television set was precariously perched on a shelf across the far corner of the ward, and there were stiff vases of flowers set on tables spaced at intervals down the middle of the room. I looked at my watch and wondered if I had time for a cup of coffee and a couple of doughnuts at the Institute if I left straight away. On the other hand, it was pleasant to sit beside such a very good-looking man as his sole visitor. Anyone glancing down the ward casually just scanning the beds would think that I had a right to be there, and that we knew each other. The idea didn't displease me.

I studied him. He was older than I had thought at first, maybe twenty-eight or nine. His eyes flickered open and remained at half mast. I indicated the basket of fruit, still in its red cellophane wrapping.

'Did your landlady bring that in for you?'

Vivacity returned to his face and voice for a moment. 'Mrs. Burroughs's nickname is The

Adding Machine. She believes in three references, a month's rent in advane, no smoking, drinking or visitors of the opposite sex, and that Charity Begins at Home. I'll probably have to clear out and find somewhere else to live after this.'

'But you'll need one or two things while you're in here.' Someone had shaved him, but he wore hospital pyjamas. 'What about pyjamas, shaving things . . . surely she must . . . ?'

'I doubt it. My boss, Mr. Brenner, would get them for me, but he left today for the Aegean. He couldn't delay his departure, and he'll be away a minimum of two weeks, maybe longer.'

'I'll get them for you,' I said, and then flushed, realising how I'd risked a snub.

'Would you?' He wasn't going to snub me; he was surprised, but delighted. 'No—why should you?'

'I don't mind. That is—if it's not too far away, and your landlady wouldn't mind?'

'Egerton Gardens, Number 10. Just off the Common. She's always there in the evenings, but if you were to phone first . . .'

'All right, then. I'll do it!' What a pleasure it was to do something for someone else! He was smiling, too, as his eyelids quivered shut again.

'You did say your name was Sue, didn't you? Mine's Charles—Charles Ashton. Remind me to thank you properly some time for saving my life twice over.'

'Oh, that!' I don't think he heard me. His eyelids were fast shut. There was a slight mark at the corner of his mouth, but otherwise his face hadn't been touched. I wondered why. I shifted in my seat, and at once his eyelids jumped. It was only half past seven, and it would take me just five minutes to get to the Institute for my evening class. I made myself comfortable in my chair.

A young woman across the ward leaned over and embraced a patient; he held her tightly and returned her kiss. She straightened up, laughing and pushed her hair back into place, glancing around with a half-guilty, half-satisfied expression to see if anyone had noticed. She caught my eye on her. I looked down, thinking how embarrassed I would have felt if I had been caught kissing someone in public like that, and then remembered that two years ago I had thought nothing of greeting Rob in just such a way. Why not? We'd spoken of marriage, we'd made love . . . and then I'd missed a period and he feared I was pregnant. By the time the trouble had been traced to some pills I'd been taking for slimming purposes, he'd turned his eyes elsewhere. I didn't particularly want to think about him. I wished I hadn't come.

Automatically my hand moved to the box of chocolates on the bed, and in passing touched Charles' hand. It was almost accidental, but not quite. I think I'd wanted to show the girl across the ward that she was not the only one to be able to lay claim to a man. I took my hand away, and was amazed to see Charles open his own hand, and leave it there, palm uppermost on the coverlet. I stared at it, wondering if he meant some insult by the gesture, and then placed my hand squarely on his, feeling that it served me right if he did. His fingers folded firmly over mine. His hand was too warm; he would be running a temperature, no doubt. Probably didn't even know what he was doing. Nevertheless, I didn't attempt to remove my hand.

My eyes went to the basket of fruit once more, and I wondered if his girl-friend had sent it to him. He was accepting me as a substitute for her, no doubt. I started on a sigh, and then controlled it so as not to disturb him. The odd thing was that now everyone could see that I, plain Sue was holding the hand of an exceedingly good-looking man, I didn't feel the need to look around and check that they had registered the fact. I was quite content to sit there and look at Charles and at our linked hands, and just occasionally, at my watch.

'We used to call her Black-eyed Susan,' he said conversationally, without warning. His eyes were still closed, but he was talking to me and not to himself. 'And then, when she'd lost most of her paint we used to call her just Sue.

17

She was David's doll, really, that he bought in a jumble sale, but he didn't mind us joining in his games. She was the Princess who had to be rescued from the Dragon, and the Lady of Shalott when we played down by the river, and Maid Marian and even Peter Pan when David made a harness for her so that she could fly. Ronald said she was better than a girl to play with, because she didn't answer back.'

'All boys?' I prompted. 'No girls?'

'Three boys—David's the eldest, then Ronald and me. No girls. Poor Dad—he did so want a girl. But Mother wouldn't have liked girls, not really.'

I made a note of that fact that he called his mother 'Mother', and his father 'Dad'. Interesting. There was a reddened band of skin round his wrist that was interesting, too. He fell silent, and I thought he'd gone to sleep. The hands of my watch crept round far too fast. At five to eight I stood up with some reluctance, and withdrew my hand. His head had slanted towards me on the pillow. I thought he'd dozed off, but when I moved, he jerked his eyelids open again.

'I must go,' I said. 'But I'll come back and bring those things for you tomorrow.'

He nodded fractionally and I left, quite forgetting my box of chocolates. I stopped on the way out to check on the visiting hours for the following day. I was going to be late for my evening class, but who cared?

Bessie could hardly wait for the lunch hour to receive my report, and was annoyed that I said I had to rush my food.

'Got to dash to collect my winter coat,' I explained, refusing a pudding. 'So that I can go to his landlady's before I go to see him again.' I told her the story he'd given me, and was amused to see that she accepted his explanation of temporary amnesia.

'It must have been one helluva party,' she mused. 'I expect they all got tight, tried to do something silly, this lad of yours got hurt, they panicked, and were taking him home when the car crashed and they left him for someone else to pick up.'

'He's not that young,' I said, scraping my plate. 'Late twenties? A bit late for that sort of wild party. And he's got red marks round his wrists as if he'd been tied up at some point. I didn't notice them when I found him, but I looked specially last night.'

'You're imagining things. I expect there's a perfectly good explanation for his injuries.'

'He's well-educated,' I said thoughtfully, 'intelligent, quick-witted . . . a bit on the thin side, but not dissipated. I don't think it's drugs . . .'

'What?'

'Something's wrong,' I said, pushing my

19

plate away from me. 'Maybe I'll find out more this evening.'

I found Mrs. Burroughs's without difficulty, and as I scanned the front of it, a slight, dark-haired young man ran up the steps and began to fidget in his pockets for his keys.

'Can I help you?' he asked, inquisitive as a squirrel.

I told him I'd come to collect one or two things for Mr. Ashton, who was in hospital, and he was all over me. He was a nice lad, without a mite of ill-nature in him.

'Poor Charles, of course! Come on in, and I'll locate the Terror of Egerton Gardens for you. Mind the lino—polishing day today, and I've cracked my ankle twice against that hat-stand on polishing days . . that's it! Like playing Shipwreck in this hall, leaping from mat to mat. I really must get along to see Charles. Do you know how long he's in for? Could have knocked me down with a feather when old Mrs. B. told us what had happened. I mean . . . Charles! Who'd have thought it of the old sober-sides? Now me or old John in Number Three—yes! Any day or night, if you get my meaning, but for Charles to go to a wild party and then crash his car . . . The notion takes some swallowing. And his car in dock, too? I'd never have thought, from the way he looked after it, that he'd let it stand outside in the rain all night, let alone crash it.'

He paused to take breath as he knocked on

20

a heavy door at the foot of the stairs.

'Mrs. Burroughs! Someone to collect Charles' things to take to the hospital.'

From inside the room martial music announced Newstime on television. The door opened and a majestic, calm-faced woman appeared.

'I'm glad to hear it,' she announced. 'Mr. Bessiter, take the young lady upstairs and see that she removes all of Mr. Ashton's belongings; they are all packed up ready for her. I have placed an envelope containing a rebate on Mr. Ashton's rent inside his suitcase. Naturally he will not be returning here.'

'But . . .' I said. The door closed with finality. One did not argue with Mrs. Burroughs. The friendly lad beside me tugged at my arm, and gestured towards the stairs.

'No use arguing, my dear. Newstime is sacrosanct. Poor old Charles! He does like his nosh and she serves up a decent-sized plateful. Wonder where he'll go? I'll suppose he'll go back home, but he always swore he'd sooner starve, and of course he could afford to get a proper flat, but . . . Maybe there'd be room for him at my married sister's till he gets something permanent. Or did his boss . . . yes, I expect he'll go to Whitestones—lucky dog! No, wait a minute, he can't do that, if Mr. Brenner's away. Or could he? Maybe I'd better see if I can turn up somewhere for him, so when you see him tonight, you'd better ask him what he wants to do.'

He showed me into a big room, overlooking the front. It was pleasantly furnished. A big desk in the bay window lay open, divested of papers. Wardrobe doors hung slightly ajar, and the bed had already been stripped. A large suitcase lay near the door, together with a cardboard box of shoes and a canvas grip bulging with books and sweaters.

'Look,' I said, 'I only wanted his toilet things. Could you help me find them?'

'But he's got them with him!' said Mr. Bessiter. 'He came back for his leather holdall on Friday night—about eight o'clock it would be, because Mrs. B. was furious that he hadn't told her he wouldn't be in for supper. He said he'd to go away for the night, unexpectedly. He often did, you know, with his boss. Here, there and everywhere at a moment's notice. Nothing unusual in that. Or he might have been going home for the weekend—I went with him once—fine place, they did have a lot of money you know, and they still keep it up even though . . . but he wouldn't want me to talk about that! I always wondered why he didn't commute from his home, for it's only about five miles, but he said he liked to be independent. I think his mother gets up his wick, myself, but I'm not sure I wouldn't have put up with it . . .'

'Let's get this straight. He collected things

for an overnight stay on Friday evening, and just didn't come back? But if he went home, why haven't his family missed him, or been in touch with the hospital? Did he have an overcoat with him? Was he wearing a jacket?'

'In this weather? My dear girl are you mad? And he feeling the cold as he does! Of course he was wearing a jacket with his suit, and as for an overcoat . . . well, his sheepskin-lined one isn't here, so I suppose he had that with him.' He started for the suitcase.

I stopped him. 'Can't we leave these things here until he gets out of hospital?'

'Not with Mrs. B in her present mood. Knowing her, she's already re-let the room, and if she hasn't I'll ask if I can have it, because it's much bigger than mine, and I wouldn't mind paying the extra . . .'

'But I can't take them.'

'All you've got to do is dump them at the hospital,' said Mr. Bessiter reasonably. 'They'll hold them for him till he gets out and . . . maybe I'll ring my sister tomorrow, eh? That is your Mini outside?' Still talking, he started off down the stairs. I followed with the canvas grip. 'Shame I can't come tonight with you,' he was saying. 'But it's nosh time at seven and I've got a date afterwards, but if Charles is to be in for long I could get round and see him either tomorrow or the next day. Mrs. B. said it was just a hair-line fracture he'd got and they didn't need to operate, is that right?'

As we descended the stairs, Mrs. Burroughs opened the door of her room and stood there, watching us to make sure we didn't take anything except Charles' luggage. I gave her a weak smile, which she didn't return. It was a tight squeeze, getting everything in the back of the Mini, but Mr. Bessiter helped me, jamming the box of shoes in the passenger seat, still talking. 'Hey, what's old man Brenner saying about this? Hopping mad he must be without Charles to fetch and carry for him. I wouldn't have that job for all the tea in China—told Charles so, too, but I gather there's some kind of family connection, so maybe it's all right. Say, I haven't heard him speak of you, have I? I mean, he's pretty close-mouthed when it comes to talk of the fair sex, but . . .'

'I don't really know him at all,' I said hastily. 'I just picked him up off the pavement and took him to hospital. That's all.'

That shut him up for a moment. He gave me a thoughtful stare. I told myself that I was not going to blush, and did just that very thing. I pulled the coat of my collar up to help hide my reaction; it was the one I had just collected from the cleaners and it suited my fair skin and brown hair well enough. It was more becoming than my tatty old raincoat, anyway.

' 'Bye!' he said, waving me off. 'Cross your fingers that Mrs. B will let me have his room, won't you? And tell Charles I was asking after him.'

I wondered if he'd ever get round to visiting the hospital; I didn't think he would.

The hospital wouldn't accept Charles' luggage. They said that they had no facilities for storing patients' belongings and that I must take them away again with me. A patient could bring in a certain number of items of personal property and they handed me the appropriate list—but up till the day of his departure he was not supposed to have anything else with him.

I was waiting outside the doors of the ward as the hands of the clock ticked up to seven, and was one of the first through. I could see Charles' head turned towards the doors in anticipation of my coming, and it gave me a thrill to realise that he was waiting for me and no one else.

'Hello!' I said, and plumped myself down in the chair at his bedside. He was looking less heavy-eyed than on the previous evening, and he was a better colour. His eyes were properly open, and he managed a smile, if a constrained one. I picked up his air of constraint at once, and being me I put it down to dislike of my presence. At once I felt drab and fat; I started to fidget in my pockets for the odd half bar of chocolate, until I realised that my coat was fresh from the cleaners, and there wasn't likely to be any store of food in it.

I thought I'd better make some excuse to get away early; I'd tell him about the luggage, and then disappear. If I were quick, I might get to the ABC in time for a snack before the main film.

'How are you feeling?' I asked, thinking that it was only polite to ask.

'Do you want the official hospital version, or my own impressions?'

'Your own impressions, please!' I nearly laughed. Whatever the reason for his constraint, it could not be me, for he had set himself to entertain.

'Well, I've got a cracking headache on and off, I still can't remember anything after last Friday night, I'm so strung up with bandages and harnesses that I feel like a badly-wrapped Christmas parcel, and I shan't have the full use of my left hand for some time to come. Satisfied?'

'You're much better. Much. I'm so glad.'

To my amazement he half closed his eyes and began to redden. His right hand clenched and fidgeted on the bed near me. 'I'm sorry about last night,' he said. 'Hanging on to you like a two-year-old! What you must have thought . . .'

'Oh,' I said, as red in the face as he. 'That! Well—I didn't mind that at all.'

'A complete stranger to you . . . a fully-grown man . . . !'

'You just needed someone to hang on to,' I

said hastily. 'A sort of mother substitute. Probably my being called Susan had something to do with it. A transference of childhood memories . . . ?'

'A mother substitute!' He gave a crack of laughter and then winced. 'Remind me not to laugh, will you? They say I've only got two cracked ribs, but it feels more like the lot gone at times.'

'Who did you get across to come by such a beating-up?'

He stared at me without a smile. His nose looked pinched, and the bosses of his cheekbones stood out. He was a big-boned man, but far too thin.

'I'm sorry,' I said. 'I forgot you said you couldn't remember.'

'All hysteria,' he said, speaking lightly, as if used to giving this particular alibi. His eyes were watchful. 'The doctor says I'm deliberately suppressing the memory of what happened because of the nature of my injuries. The police are in two minds about what happened. Either I was flagged down by hitch-hikers, beaten up and robbed, or I was so drunk I got into a fight with someone, drove away still drunk and then crashed the car to complete the picture.'

'You weren't driving.'

'Why do you say that?'

I told him why. I told him what I'd seen on the night I'd found him, and of the odd behaviour of the second car, as well.

'Would you recognise either the man or the woman whom you say were driving my car, if you saw them again?'

'I don't know. I shouldn't think so. I only saw them for a second or two, either time.'

He relaxed. I guessed he'd been worried that I could have identified them to the police.

'But you know who they were,' I said. 'Your friend Mr. Bessiter told me you left work, got back to the boarding-house, properly dressed, about eight. You collected some things for an unexpected overnight stay, put them into your leather holdall, apologised to Mrs. Burroughs for missing supper and took off again. He thinks you went back to work, or that you went home.'

'Neither. J.B. and I had had words that day. Nothing unusual, but I wouldn't have gone crawling back so quickly.'

'Words about what?'

'Not what you'd call a quarrel. He was pressing me to go with him on this trip, but I wanted some time to myself, and refused. Then he tried to get me to promise I'd move in with him when he got back, but . . .' He smiled, deliberately employing charm. 'Leave it, will you? I feel far too fragile for post mortems.'

'Charm will get you nowhere,' I said austerely.

'Christ! You sound just like J.B. " Facts,

28

Charles not feelings!"'

'Yes, let's get at the facts, shall we? If you didn't go back to work, then you must have gone home. I've a good mind to ring your people . . .'

'They know nothing about this, and I couldn't have gone home last weekend because there was no one there. Mother was away staying with friends, and Ronald and Jane were at her people's. There wouldn't have been anyone there.'

'Your elder brother—David?'

'In Northern Ireland, defusing bombs and collecting scars.' He smiled at my expression of alarm. 'Just one little one across his eyebrow.'

'Your father, then?'

'In jail, where he's been for the last six months.'

There was a nasty pause. Out of nervousness I did the wrong thing. I laughed as if he'd made a joke. 'Oh, really?'

'Oh, really!' he repeated, but his tone was biting, and his lips thin.

'I'm sorry. It was just that it was so unexpected.'

'To us, too.'

'What did he . . . ?'

'Fraudulent conversion, for which he got seven years. He is an accountant, like myself and Ronald.' Again those thin lips held firm against pain; I felt I'd touched not just a raw spot, but an open wound. He was far too thin, and probably lived on his nerves. I looked away, trying to reduce tension.

'I wish you'd leave it alone,' he said. 'I told the police it must have been some hitch-hikers who went too far . . .'

'They'd have taken your car as well, if they were just out to rob you. You say they took your jacket and your overnight things, and left you your car?'

'Well, they crashed it, didn't they? And someone was bound to come along the road . . .'

'You'd shaved that day,' I said. 'You went off, of your own free will, on Friday evening, to stay with someone you knew. You were with them until late Monday night, when they tied you up, tortured you and then threw you out on the road to die.'

He wasn't going to admit it, but he wasn't going to lie again, either. He was exhausted. I found I was holding his hand in both of mine. It felt warm, but not as warm as it had done the other night. I lowered my eyes to his hand, lifted the sleeve of his pyjama to touch the fast-fading burn mark round his wrist, checked to see that he was watching, and replaced the sleeve.

'So why hasn't your family visited you?' I asked.

'I told Sister they were away. I don't want them worried. I'll be out of here by the end of the week. I'm walking wounded now.'

'You've no money nowhere to go. I've got your luggage because Mrs. Burroughs has thrown you out. Your friend Mr. Bessiter said he'd find you somewhere to stay, but I think . . .'

'Don't think any more, Sue,' he said, and removed his hand from mine. His eyes were wide. 'Just forget about it, and me. Understand?'

The bell shrilled, announcing the end of Visiting Hour. A nurse switched on the television set at the far end of the ward. Visitors bustled between beds and back to the outside world.

'That's it, then,' I said, getting up and digging my hands deep into my pockets. I felt like crying. 'Hope there's something good on the telly for you.'

He turned his head fractionally to glance at it. 'That? Too far away for me to see properly, without my glasses.'

'You wear glasses for driving? That proves you weren't driving at the time of the crash, for you weren't wearing glasses when I found you, and they weren't loose in the car, either.'

'No doubt the hitch-hikers fancied them,' he said, smiling. It wasn't a great effort, as smiles went, but I gave him full marks for trying.

'Liar!' I said, and stalked off down the ward. The girl from the bed opposite Charles

31

caught up with me as I left.

'It's horrid leaving them in here and going home by ourselves, isn't it?' she said. 'I can't wait to get him out of there and fuss him up a little.'

I nodded agreement. I felt exactly the same way about Charles, only I didn't suppose I'd ever see him again.

CHAPTER TWO

'What do you know, if anything, about a Mr. John Brenner?' I asked our Company Secretary at coffee-time next day. He knew plenty.

Charles' boss was some sort of financial wizard, one of the grey men who had advised the last Government on international finance. He had holdings in one or two companies in the town, but this was more to keep his hand in now that he'd officially retired, than because he was interested in their well-being. He was reputed to be a millionaire. He lived in a show place called Whitestones, just outside town, and he had at least two Rolls-Royces with telephones in them; he also had a chauffeur, a living-in staff, and kept a yacht in the Mediterranean. He had been seriously ill some time ago, but appeared to have recovered. His picture had appeared in the local paper on occasions when he was guest of honour at some function or other.

My informant also said that in his opinion, and strictly off the record, John Brenner was a bastard of the first water, and that he only kept his staff by paying them fabulous salaries. In his private life he was supposed to be about as human as a computer.

' "Facts, not feelings",' I murmured, trailing back to my own office.

'How's Handsome?' enquired Bessie.

'Got a skin too few, I'd say. And terribly thin.' I told her what I'd learned the previous night from Mr. Bessiter, but I didn't tell her what I'd deduced from it, or of my subsequent argument with Charles.

'Now's your chance,' said Bessie. 'Kidnap him and take him off to your lair while he's still groggy from the anaesthetic.'

'Mm?' I said, thinking it was odd that if Charles could remember what had happened to him, and where he'd left his belongings, he'd sent me off to Mrs. Burroughs to look for them.

'That flat opposite yours—isn't it to let again? Put him in there, and Bob's Your Uncle.'

I grunted. I lived in a big old Victorian house, which was divided up into two flats on each floor, each complete with kitchen, large bedsitting-room, and tiny hall. There was a bathroom on each landing. My flat was on the top floor, and the one opposite me had been empty for some time following a thunderstorm during which rain had poured in over the occupant of the bed. The agents had told me that morning that officially the flat was to be redecorated before it was relet, but that it might be possible for me to have it for a friend on a week to week basis. I thought about the palatial Whitestones, and Charles' home, which was reported to be "a fine place". I didn't think Charles would like what I had to offer.

'When you see him tonight,' said Bessie, 'you can ask him, can't you?'

'Oh, I'm not seeing him again,' I said, and began to talk about the picture at the ABC which I wanted to see instead. I spent a miserable evening, chewing toffees and thinking about my long-lost Rob and about Charles. I was sure Charles was mixed up in something nasty, but I couldn't believe that he was a villain himself. Of course, I didn't know what a villain should look like. I just had a feeling that he wasn't one.

Like Charles, I went by feelings, and not by facts. Except . . .

There was something bothering me. Charles had as good as told me not to go and see him again, but he hadn't asked where I lived, or made any request about the disposal of his luggage. Was he leaving the door open for me to go and see him again, or had he just forgotten?

The police were at my flat when I got back, asking for a statement about the accident. I told them what I knew. They seemed set on the theory that Charles had been beaten up and robbed by hitch-hikers, and I didn't see any necessity to query it. They said I'd probably saved his life, which was nice of them, if not entirely accurate.

The next morning I woke with a firm determination to put him out of my mind. I would phone Mrs. Burroughs, get Mr. Bessiter's work phone number, and confirm that Charles had been fixed up with accommodation; then I would drop Charles a note telling him where to collect his luggage, and that would be that.

Mr. Bessiter was only a trifle less loquacious on the phone than when we had met. He hadn't done anything about finding a room for Charles, but he'd visited him the previous night in hospital and found him 'surprisingly chirpy'. He told me Charles had decided he would have to return home for the rest of his fortnight's leave, and that he'd be phoning his brother to collect him from hospital, either on Friday or Saturday morning.

'What about his luggage?' I asked.

'Didn't mention it, love. I suppose he'll be phoning you about it.'

'He doesn't have my phone number or my

address.'

'He'll contact you somehow. Very capable guy, our Charles. Well, must dash—work calls, and all that. Cheers!'

Bessie came to lunch with a frown. 'This Ashton,' she said, picking at her food. 'I don't know if it's the same family, but a friend of my aunt's lost a lot of money when a man called Ashton was prosecuted for fraud. You did say your chap was an accountant, didn't you?'

'It's the same one,' I said, reaching for a bread roll.

'Well,' said Bessie, 'I wouldn't have anything more to do with him, if I were you.' She said she'd been telling her mother about my little adventure, and her mother had got on the phone to her aunt, and obtained the story from her. The Ashtons had been chartered accountants for three generations, and were a highly respected family. Oliver Ashton, the father, had been popular and had done a lot of charity work, which made it all the more astounding when he was arrested, charged and sentenced for fraud.

Apparently he had suggested to one or two of his clients that they might care to invest in certain blue chip securities, and had asked them to send their cheques made out to him personally, rather than to the firm. Time passed, but the clients received neither their share certificates, nor dividends for the money they had handed over. The money had vanished as soon as it reached Oliver Ashton. The prosecution case was that he had diverted the money partly for his own use, and partly to bolster up his wife's private company, Collett Cosmetics. Some of the money had turned up in a private bank account of Oliver Ashton's, but the bulk of it had never been recovered, and he had refused to reveal what he'd done with it. There had been no apparent reason why a respected chartered accountant should suddenly have taken to fiddling the books, but there was no doubt that he had done so. He had pleaded guilty, been sentenced, and the family firm passed into other hands.

'Anything else?' I asked, although I didn't really want to hear.

'Not much. One of the sons is supposed to be brilliant—double first or something, but he's well out of it, working in London. She— my aunt—thinks the son who worked with his father in the family firm is now more or less on the breadline, working for a pittance in a sinecure found for him by family connections. I don't know anything else.'

It was more than enough. I assumed that it was Charles who had worked for his father, and I spent most of the rest of the day wondering if he had been involved in the fraud or not. I thought it was very odd, to say the least, that Charles had been connected with one case of fraud, was now working for a very rich man, and had recently been beaten up.

Both Bessie and Charles had advised me to keep away from him. I would just go to the hospital to tell him where to find his luggage when he needed it, and that would be that.

He wasn't expecting me. I could see his bright head as soon as I entered the ward. His bed was now next to that at which the affectionate young girl was a visitor. He was sitting upright, and trying to write with a left hand free of bandages, but still bound round with strapping. There was an air of tension, almost of fierceness about the way he looked; I wondered if he'd lost weight again.

'Hello,' I said, keeping my hands deep in my pockets. His eyes and mouth flicked into a welcome before he could control himself.

'Sue!' Then he had himself in hand again, and the smile was gone. 'Nice of you to come, but as you can see, I'm getting on well now. I'll be out tomorrow or the next day.'

'Left-handed, are you? I wondered why they'd concentrated on that hand.'

He slid the letter under his pad, his eyes wary. I found I was enjoying our clash of wits.

'It was nothing but a rough-house that went too far. Nothing would have happened if I hadn't lost my temper and fought back. Everyone is very apologetic about it, and it won't happen again. So let's forget about it, shall we?'

I saw that there was now a gold pencil and a

good quality handkerchief on the top of his locker, with a paperback. A nice-looking grey jacket swung on a hook at the back of his locker, and I guessed his leather grip would be inside.

'I'm so glad you've stopped having amnesia,' I said affably. 'It must have been wearing, trying to remember which lies you've told to whom. And have your "friends" recovered your car, as well as returning your belongings?'

'Yes. It's at the Blue Star Garage. All's well that ends well.'

'Except that you've lost your digs, had a week in hospital, and are still in pain.'

'You've got it all wrong. I've known these people for years. It was a drunken frolic that got out of hand. It was quite accidental that I got knocked out, and I don't really blame them for panicking afterwards. It would be absurd to charge them with grievous bodily harm, when I have to go on working with them, and . . . anyway, they didn't get off lightly. One man's got a cracked kneecap and the other's still sporting a black eye.' Satisfaction oiled his voice, and I smiled involuntarily. He twitched me a grin. 'Simmer down, Sue! They're falling over themselves with apologies, paying for my car to be put right, buying me a radio to go in it by way of compensation. They've also offered to put me up.'

'Like the curate's egg,' I commented. 'Good in parts. You're an awfully good liar, aren't you?' He opened his mouth to refute the charge, but by the quick snap of his eyelids I guessed I wouldn't get the truth. 'Don't!' I said. 'If you don't want to tell me the truth, all right; I suppose you've got your own reasons. But don't lie.'

He grinned at me, acknowledging guilt, and didn't volunteer any more information. I realised I'd been standing since I came in, and hooked forward a chair.

'Your luggage is at my place when you want it. Number 10, Queens Gardens, top floor. Shall I post that letter for you?'

'No, I haven't finished it yet. I have to let my boss know when I'll be fit to fly out to him. I suppose I'll have to go.'

'Do you lie to him, too?'

'Not the way you mean. We lie like the devil to each other, but it's . . .'

'A sort of game?'

'Yes, we both know the rules.' We were like two fencers, circling each other; he was telling me a great deal about himself all the time. The picture he was giving me of his relationship with John Brenner hardly matched the one given me by our Company Secretary, and yet I preferred Charles' version.

'Will you move into Whitestones when you get back?' I asked.

'Maybe I'll have to, for a while. He has a staff of four living in already, so my presence wouldn't make much difference, but . . . I like to be independent.'

'You could do with fattening up.'

'I eat enough, but seem to burn it up. I've dropped nearly a stone this last six months.'

Six months. Since his father was convicted.

'Why don't you go back home, then?'

'Most unrestful. Mother lives in the centre of a well-organised whirlwind and in any case doesn't tolerate weakness in her sons. She's incapable of allowing anyone except Jane that's my sister-in-law—to sit down and rest while she's working, and she herself works a twelve hour day. She has her own firm, you know—Collett Cosmetics. Ronald works for her and I don't know how he stands it. Jane's not strong; she's expecting a baby, and . . . I'll find somewhere quiet where I can be on my own for a week or ten days. I had intended driving North to visit some friends, but that's out now. Then I'll join J.B. on the yacht. I'll see what happens after that.'

'You told Mr. Bessiter you planned to go home.'

'He's got a loose tongue in his head. I need somewhere quiet where nobody will fuss over me.'

I crossed the fingers of both hands, took a deep breath, and told myself that a snub wouldn't kill me. 'I don't suppose you'd be

41

interested,' I said, 'but there's a flatlet going in the house in which I live.' I told him about it, warning him it was in bad decorative order, that it wasn't particularly well furnished, that there was no garage or cooking, or services laid on. I said I could perhaps give him the odd meal, if he felt like it. I ended up mumbling into my coat collar, expecting him to interrupt at any moment to say he wasn't interested, thank you. When I finished, I found he was staring at me as if I'd offered him a room at The Hilton.

'Just for a week?' I said, beginning to hope. 'And you do need fattening up. I can be your reference. The landlord would need a week's rent in advance, but . . .'

'Oh, Sue!' Somehow his hand was holding mine as tightly as ever. 'If you were to get involved, I'd never forgive myself.'

I sat there smiling, thinking I'd be able to make excuses to see him often during the coming week, and that maybe he'd even continue to see me afterwards.

'I don't know what time they'll let me out tomorrow, if they do. Number 10, Queens Gardens? I'll take a taxi . . .'

'No, you'll feel groggy on your first day out. You phone me when you're let out, and I'll collect you.'

His hand was cool in mine, tonight. A movement from the next bed caught my eye, and I glanced up to see the girl visiting there was in tears.

'Industrial injury,' explained Charles. 'They hoped they wouldn't have to amputate, but it doesn't look as if he's going to get away with it.'

'That's terrible,' I said, clasping his hand as if to make sure nobody whipped him away to operate while I was there.

'Yes,' said Charles, watching my face in a way I couldn't interpret. The bell for the end of Visiting Hour rang, and the girl next door flung her arms round her boy-friend, sobbing. I met Charles' eye, and coloured up. The urge to bend over and kiss him was strong, but I made myself step away as I stood up. Did his face betray disappointment? Had he pulled just slightly—on my hand as I rose?

I hesitated. 'That first day—why did you send me to Mrs. Burroughs's to look for your shaving things, when you knew they weren't there?'

'I was confused,' he said, looking innocent. 'The knock on my head—I didn't know how much or how little I could say to you.'

'And your luggage? Why did you tell me not to come again, but forgot to ask for my address?'

'You know perfectly well why. I wanted you to have an excuse to come back.'

I had suspected it, but hadn't allowed myself to believe in it. I turned and walked out of the ward without another word, on the heels of the girl from the next bed. She was crying. I felt immensely sorry for her, and offered her a lift home. She lived the other side of town, but I didn't mind, I was feeling so elated.

'Do you go every night?' I asked idly. 'It's a long way.'

'Every night that I can. He just sits there watching the door if I don't go; even when he knows that I can't possibly make it. Like your chap did last night.'

'Did he?' I couldn't have been more gratified. 'But he had another visitor last night.'

'Three. The first two didn't stay long. They were more like business acquaintances, if you know what I mean. He had longish fair hair fairer than your chap's, and was very tall, and thin with dark glasses. He brought some clothes in a bag, talked a while, and then left. His wife was odd, though. She didn't say a word all the time they were there—just sat there smiling at nothing. She was wearing a super trouser suit.'

'Was she wearing a red scarf?'

'No. Do you know them?'

'I don't think so. Did the man limp?'

'No, but I thought he was hiding a black eye behind those glasses. Did your chap give it to him? I thought they acted a bit cool. But the other fellow who came was ever so nice; he gave my Tom some cigarettes and wanted to fetch some beer in for us all, but of course Sister wouldn't have allowed that.'

I had no difficulty in identifying Mr. Bessiter as the second visitor.

'Your man still looked for you, though. All the time the second chap was talking—and he hardly stopped—your man was checking to see who came in, every time the door opened. Tom said he knew just how he was feeling, and we were ever so glad to see you come again tonight.'

'Thanks for telling me,' I said. The news was worth the inconvenience of giving her a lift.

*   *   *

By the time I got Charles home, he was shivering. A big man, he was half a head taller than me; I'm well built with it, and he was far too thin.

'Where's your overcoat?' I asked, for he wasn't wearing one.

'I left it at Whitestones. That's how J.B. knew I was in trouble. He knew I might walk out on him, but I wouldn't go off without my overcoat in this weather.'

I'd unpacked for him. He didn't have many clothes, and hardly any personal effects; no photographs, old theatre bills, bank statements or letters. Just a few receipted bills from his garage. He didn't even blink at the

45

barely furnished room, but expressed himself more than satisfied. I thought of the meagre bed coverings, and wondered how he'd manage at night, if he felt the cold.

'Have a cup of coffee on me to start with?' I said, and showed him across the landing into my flat, which was warm and well-furnished. I'd gone without a holiday the previous year in order to lay down a good quality yellow carpet from wall to wall, I'd put up new curtains to match, and covered the bed-settee and armchairs in gay-patterned material. He liked it, I could tell. He wandered around, fingering things, taking books out of place, glancing through them, and putting them back, shifting things. I laughed aloud, thinking of my mother's dictum that men were perfectly all right in the abstract, but when they were underfoot, they were inclined to make nuisances of themselves.

'Yes?' he asked, and then, seriously, 'It's only a very slight risk, you know. They don't need to see me again until J.B. gets back.'

I very nearly told him that I thought he was worth more than a slight risk, but offered coffee instead. He sat down, switched on the telly, and asked if I'd get him a *Financial Times* when I went shopping. He'd moved in.

He hardly moved from my best armchair all day, except when I dragged him out for a short walk in the afternoon. He made no attempt to return to his own room, and I certainly wasn't

46

pushing him out. I cooked, he washed up as to the manner born, we chatted of this and that, I sewed a button on his shirt, he cleaned my shoes. I found myself singing, twice.

Then Rita came in to borrow some mugs for a party they were having that night in the ground floor flat, and for a moment I thought I'd lost him. Rita had long legs, a model figure, false eyelashes and although she had plenty of money, didn't appear to hold any job for long. I didn't like her, and she usually ignored me unless she wanted something. This time she saw Charles and wanted him to appear at her party. He declined, saying he was only just out of hospital and couldn't manage the stairs. She said he could put his arm round her shoulders and she'd help him down, and as she said it, she wiggled her hips suggestively.

'Broken collar-bone,' said Charles, not moving. 'But why don't you go, Sue? No need for you to stay to look after me.'

That wasn't what Rita had had in mind at all. I put her out of her misery, saying I wanted an early night, and as she left Charles treated me to a grin to show that he was pleased that I'd refused.

'That type bores me,' he explained, adjusting the picture on the television set. I wondered exactly how much wool it would take to knit him a sweater.

I woke with a start, and sat upright, shivering. It was two o'clock of a dark winter's night, and very cold. I pulled the bedclothes around me, and wondered how Charles was faring.

'No!' There it came again, that cry. I switched on my light, and listened. Another few minutes and I thought I must have been mistaken. Then it came again; a cry of protest, or possibly of despair.

I slipped across the landing and knocked on Charles' door. The big house lay quiet below—even the party in Rita's flat had subsided to a grumble. Charles hadn't locked the door. I slipped in. He had left the reading lamp on, with a shirt thrown across it to dim the light. He was in the grip of a nightmare, with half the bedclothes on the floor. He was turning his head from side to side, obviously in pain. He wasn't wearing pyjamas, and now I could see exactly how much strapping they had needed to hold broken and cracked bones into place. Sweat stood out on his forehead, in spite of the cold.

I caught his hand and spoke his name. He started awake, breathing shallowly. I held his hand until I was sure he was fully out of his nightmare, and when I released it, he put it to his forehead. I guessed at a headache. I pulled the bedcothes up over him; he'd put a couple of sweaters on top of the clothes, but he was by no means warm. At this rate he'd get pneumonia and end back in hospital.

'Aspirins?' I asked. 'You've got some pain-killers from the hospital?'

He shook his head, screwing up his eyes.

'I've got some,' I said, and made my way back to my room. I lit the gas-fire and thought I'd better light his, too. He'd probably been reliving the experiences of the previous weekend in his nightmare. When I turned round, he was in the doorway, a short towelling bathrobe round him, blinking.

'I'll sit up for a while,' he said. 'I don't want another nightmare like that.'

I watched him take the aspirins. I knew he wouldn't step over the threshold of my room unless I invited him to do so, not at night. I told myself to be careful, and that I knew nothing good of him. On the other hand, if I did invite him in, and we did get to sleep together, he would be more likely to give me his company during the coming week.

'Come on in,' I said, pulling at his sleeve. 'I'll see you don't have bad dreams in here. Besides, it's too cold for you in that room.' I pushed him towards my bed and surprisingly enough he went without argument. I turned out the light, but left the gas-fire on. I slid in beside him and pulled up the covers; he hadn't taken his kimono off, and he was very tense.

'Come,' I said. 'Let me get you warm again.'

His response delighted me. He unbuttoned

my pyjamas and laid his cheek first against one breast and then the other. 'Sweet Sue!' he said. 'Sweet Sue!' It seemed to be enough for him. I lay there smiling into the half dark and felt the rhythm of his breathing slow into sleep.

I woke in the morning only when he placed a cup of coffee at my bedside and called my name.

'Sugar? I can't remember how many.' He had shaved, washed and dressed in casual clothes. His eyes were now warm and now chill.

'What is it?' He had drawn back the curtains and tidied the room. It was nearly ten o'clock of a dark Sunday morning.

'I must find somewhere else. I can't stay now.' He put out a hand to touch my cheek. 'Don't cry, Sue. You must see I can't stay now.'

'I don't see why not.'

'Because I want you—all the way.'

'Is that all? Well, what do you think I brought you home for?'

He shouted with laughter, and I grinned up at him, almost sure of myself for once.

'No, but . . . darling Sue! You know I'm in the middle of something . . .'

'Just for one week, until you have to join your boss?'

'One week.' His eyes were hungry. I started to fold back my pyjama tops, knowing that he did at least appreciate some part of me. 'Sue, stop it!' His voice was as shaky as his hands as he tried to pull the material back over my breasts. 'You're trying to seduce me!'

'I think I'm succeeding,' I said, giggling. In the struggle that followed he ended up lying on the bed with me.

'Let's be sensible,' he begged. 'Drink your coffee, and we'll talk about it.'

'Afterwards,' I said, pulling his sweater over his head. 'Let's get our priorities in the right order.'

*   *   *

So he stayed. He put on weight, and I lost it. He mended everything in the flat that was broken, over-hauled the engine on my car and replaced the door handle. He would have redecorated the kitchen if I'd let him. He was autocratic, jealous, and demanding. Towards the end of the week he began to show flashes of hard-driving energy which left me standing.

We talked of our 'need' for each other, but never of 'love', even though I knew I was hard hit by Sunday night. We watched each other, probing to see what each was made of. We talked about ourselves mostly about childhood and our families. We talked of books and films and cabbages and kings. We talked, and ate, and slept in each other's arms. He used the room he'd rented only to keep his clothes in, and I sponged him down in the bathroom morning and night because he couldn't have a bath until all his strapping had been removed.

I told him all about my father, who was an electrical contractor with his own small business, and about my mother, who baked her own bread. I even told him, by way of a joke against me, about my first love affair. His only comment about that was to ask me if I were on the pill now. I said I wasn't, and blushed. He looked thoughtful, but didn't start taking precautions, which made me thoughtful in turn.

He talked freely about his life until he'd qualified, but little about his present job. He talked a lot about his brothers. Fair-headed, steady, short-sighted Ronald was only a year older than Charles and had acted as a brake on his younger brother's wilder impulses. Mechanically-minded David, the eldest of the three Ashton boys, was a genius with his hands and lyrically content with his flaxen Inge and three tiny daughters. He talked of his father, a gentle-mannered, kindly man, devoted to his beautiful wife Mary. He had been a butter-fingered, easy-going father, who couldn't teach his sons to play cricket because he dropped the ball all the time, but who knew the names of all the wild flowers and birds in the county. Oliver Ashton had had an operation for cancer of the lung a couple of years ago, and been a part-timer at the office

52

since then.

As for his mother, Mary Collett Ashton sounded the sort of woman you would not want for a mother-in-law; interfering, managing, spending a fortune on clothes, autocratic . . . I guessed the reason Charles didn't get on with her was because they were so much alike.

'So which of you,' I asked, 'worked in your father's office? Ronald or you?'

'Me? For Christ's sake! Can you imagine me stuck in that office with . . .? No, neither Dad nor Ronald would have stood for that. I'd have driven them mad, and I want more out of life than a career in a country . . .'

'So you're the brilliant son with the Double First and a job in London?'

'I worked for a Merchant Bank in London until just after the trial, yes.'

'So why give that up to come back here and work for John Brenner?'

'I fancied a change.'

He'd lied there. I charged him with lying, and he shrugged. Later, I asked him what he actually did at Whitestones. He smiled, employing charm. He said he licked stamps, took messages, and pasted cuttings in scrap-books. He drove his boss when the chauffeur was off duty, filed letters and made excuses if J.B. didn't want to do anything he'd promised to do.

I gave him an old-fashioned look. Charles

53

was no office boy.

'Does this sound any better?' he asked. 'I act as nursemaid. I see he takes exercise, but doesn't overdo it. I am in charge of the insulin bottles—he's a diabetic but hates to give his own injections. I chivvy him out of the house to social functions. I see he keeps in contact with his old friends, even when he curses me for doing so. I argue with him, to keep his brain keen. I go round the golf course with him, and he fines me £10 if I lose too obviously. I take him to Point to Points and place bets of sop a time for him; I see that we celebrate if he wins. I buy him Christmas presents.'

'You really care about him, then?'

He didn't want to admit it. He tried to excuse his weakness.

'J. B.'s had a raw deal in life. He and my father were at school together; my father had a happy marriage, his three sons are off his hands, and we all speak well of him both behind his back and to his face. J.B. made a disastrous marriage, his only son would spit in his face if he dared, and he was pretty much of an invalid, and a recluse by the time I got to him. He's been a power in the world, has had everything that money can buy, and there's no one but me to care if he gets indigestion or makes a killing on the Stock Market. He fears senility, incontinence; old age in the hands of servants. His son has given him no

54

grandchildren yet. I doubt if he ever will. J.B. was more or less all right while he was able to work full time, dashing around the place— lunch in Rome and dinner in Paris. Then he developed angina and was advised to retire. Inaction showed him the loneliness of his life. He degenerated physically and mentally. Twice he went into a coma because he'd neglected his injections; he's been a diabetic for years but never managed to come to terms with it. He knows perfectly well that if he doesn't take his injections on time, or if he forgets to eat, he'll be ill. But he had nothing to live for. He quarrelled with everyone; with his son, his friends . . . he couldn't keep a personal assistant longer than a month, and his servants only stay because of the fabulous salaries he pays them.'

I had never seen him so moved before. He stalked around the room, his eyes flickering this way and that, his right hand chaffing that ill-treated left hand. I felt he was on the verge of telling me something important. I kept very quiet until he went on.

'We've always seen a lot of the Brenners. David is J.B.'s god-son. He's always wanted me to work for him. ever since I was a child . . .'

He stopped abruptly, looking down at his scarred left hand. His face went blank, indicating that he was about to have a headache. I reached for the aspirins, and risked a prompt.

'Then he asked you to work for him? You were sorry for him. That's why you left your job in London to work for him?'

'No,' he said slowly, still looking at his hand. 'I could lie to you and say that that was the way it was, but it wasn't so. He didn't ask me to work for him this time. I went to him for a job. I said I wanted to study his methods so that I could learn how to make money quickly. I told him I needed a lot of money in a hurry. That was true, too, in a way. And that's as much of the truth as I can tell you, Sue.'

He took the aspirins and went to lie down. He didn't refer to the subject again.

*   *   *

Bessie was horrified on Monday, when I told her I'd left the Mini with Charles for the day. She was sure he'd disappear with the car, and that I'd never see it or him again. I defended him, saying he was going to pick me up at half past five from work. She waited with me in the hall, and tried not to crow as the minutes ticked by. Charles was five minutes late—I was to learn that he was always five minutes late for everything. Just as Bessie was urging me to phone the police, he swept in through the front door and claimed me. Wearing dark-rimmed glasses and in a huge sheepskin-lined leather coat, he looked extremely presentable.

I could see Bessie revise her opinion of him as I introduced them to each other. She even winked at me as he took my shopping basket and urged me to the door with one arm round my shoulder. His attitude was quite clear; I was his girl for the week, and I wasn't to waste time on anybody else while he was around.

I wish he could have told me I was beautiful, and ultra desirable, and all that rot, but it never seemed to occur to him to flatter me. He told me I should wear my hair loose always, that it was amazing the amount of muck some girls put on their faces, and that I wasn't to think of plucking my eyebrows. That was all the comment I got on my appearance. When I told him I feared I ought to diet, he didn't seem to understand what I was getting at. He said, shortly, that he liked something to get his hands around, and sparrow-boned females usually had sparrow-boned brains. He very nearly spanked me when I wailed that I hadn't any clothes good enough to be seen out in. He said that if my lack of good clothes bothered me that much, he'd get his mother to select something for me and he'd pay the bill. He added that he personally couldn't stand women who wore skirts so short that they showed everything they had, and necklines so low that nothing was left to the imagination. From which I gathered that he was extremely conservative as far as a woman's appearance was concerned.

He still had the occasional nightmare, but nowhere near as badly as on that first night. I would half wake him when he started to moan and shiver in his sleep, and turn him till his head rested on me, when he would quieten down and sleep through till morning. He told me he'd had nightmares once before, when he'd fallen backwards out of a tree in childhood. He still had a crescent-shaped scar on his left buttock to prove it.

After the first couple of days, he spent most of his time at Whitestones, dealing with correspondence. Once J.B. learned that Charles had not gone away, there had been a stream of cables to deal with, and Charles said he'd sooner be doing something than nothing. I found out that that was an understatement; Charles never sat down unless he'd finished doing everything he could do on his feet, and even when he did sit down, he had to have his hands occupied—with a newspaper, letters, a book. He read rapidly, extensively and comprehensively, and remembered what he'd read.

Once I came across him puzzling over a hand-drawn diagram, and was stupid enough to ask what it was all about. He said it was something his brother David had thought up, which he wanted Charles to attend to for him. He also said he'd introduce me to David when he came over on leave. He had a genius for prevarication, had Charles, but strangely enough, I always knew when he wasn't telling me the whole truth. He hadn't told me the whole truth about that diagram, for instance.

His car was ready at the end of the week, and he took me out for a meal in it into the country. The new radio was a beauty. I admired it, and was invited to try it out. I nearly blew us out of the car by turning the volume up too high. Charles said he'd really rather have had another overcoat than a radio for the car, by way of compensation, but his 'friends' had been set on the idea of a radio.

I said he ought to have more than one overcoat, anyway, and he replied that he'd sold most of his clothes and all his superfluous belongings when he left London. I didn't ask why, but I filed the reply for future reference.

Was he being blackmailed? If so, then he must have been involved in the fraud case, and was as guilty as his father. And if that was so . . . I couldn't help remembering that John Brenner was a very rich man.

I watched to see if he'd bring whisky into the flat, but he didn't. One night his friend Mr. Bessiter came round and we all went out for a drink together. Charles drank beer, and not much of that, either. I enjoyed that evening.

I didn't enjoy the speed with which the end of the week approached, though. I woke crying one night, and this time it was his turn to comfort me.

'Trust me, Sue. It's not so long now, and when it's over . . .'

'No promises,' I said, blowing my nose. 'I'm sorry I cried. I didn't mean to wake you. I told myself I was going to behave perfectly and not worry you with questions, but you know I've as much will-power as a piece of damp cotton-wool where you're concerned.'

'Define self-confidence,' he suggested.

'Something I haven't got much of?' I asked, dubiously. I felt, rather than heard him laugh against me.

'Not long now. One piece of bad luck, one piece of good. They didn't mean to give me time to think, but that's what they've done, and the *Financial Times* makes good reading nowadays. We'll soon be able to act.'

Was he considering something criminal? I didn't have any illusions about Charles. He was quite ruthless enough to think that the end justified the means.

'Whose side are you on?' I asked. 'The Baddies, or the Goodies?'

'My side,' he said, in a fierce whisper. 'I'll beat them yet.'

He pulled me to him. I couldn't struggle, without hurting him, and anyway, I didn't really want to get away. He'd been to the hospital that day to have most of his strapping removed, but he would bear the scars on his left hand until the day he died.

THREE

It had been arranged that Charles should drive down to London and then fly out to join his boss first thing on Saturday morning, so Friday was to be our last night together. He'd asked if I'd like to be taken out for the evening, but I said I'd prefer to cook him one last meal. He didn't argue; he liked my cooking so much that he said he'd recommend me for a position as a chef any time I felt like giving up my present job. I planned an extravagant, never-to-beforgotten meal.

I never did forget that night, but not because of the meal, which we hardly touched. The 'slight risk' which Charles had taken when he moved in with me turned out to be unjustifiable; or that was how Charles put it afterwards. He certainly hadn't bargained for Mr. and Mrs. Julian Brenner's descent on me when I was alone and unprepared for them.

I was mixing mayonnaise when the doorbell rang. There was a telephone-operated lock on the front door downstairs, and I thought Charles must have mislaid his keys for once. Sparing a glance at the chicken joints cooking in the oven. I sped to the phone.

'It's me!' said a man's voice plaintively. I thought Charles must have caught a cold, because his voice sounded higher than usual, but it didn't occur to me that it wasn't Charles at all. I released the door catch, and returned to the kitchen.

'Did you remember the wine?' I asked, as I heard the door of my flat open. Usually Charles came to give me a hug even before he took off his coat, but this time he didn't. I turned to see a tall, thin, flaxen-haired man usher an equally strange woman into my flat. He was wearing an expensive black overcoat, tinted glasses and a malicious smile. I didn't like the look of her, either. She was like Rita, only more so. She was slim and dark, her trouser suit would have cost me a month's salary, she had had her hair coiffured by a master, and her make-up had been copied straight from the cover of *Vogue.* A red scarf would have suited her well. I stood there with a wooden spoon in one hand, my hair hanging down my back, wearing a two-piece jersey suit which had seen better days, and with next to no make-up on. I knew that this woman and I had nothing in common, even before she opened her mouth.

'Miss Stephens?' asked the man. 'Miss Sue Stephens?'

I nodded. These must be the people who had visited Charles in hospital, and who had been responsible for his injuries; the ones Charles had not wanted me to meet.

'You don't know us, I'm afraid, but I've been hearing a fair amount about you, from a

62

mutual acquaintance.'

I didn't like to think that Charles had talked to them about me.

'Yes?' I asked, and was proud to see how steady my hand was as I put down my spoon, washed and dried my hands, and went to join them.

'Mr. Bessiter,' said the fair man. 'A charming lad—so helpful—don't you agree, Bianca? Oh, this is my wife, Bianca, I'm Julian Brenner, a friend of Charles.'

And with that he adjusted his trousers at the knee and sat down in my best chair. Bianca Brenner tested the mantelpiece for dust—there wasn't any—and perched on the edge of the table.

'Not quite what our Charles is used to,' she said. I suppose she thought that speaking in throaty tones made her sound seductive. She looked round my home, not missing the chip off the jug on the sideboard, or the stain on the carpet where I'd spilt some ink. Her eyes dissected the couch and identified it as a bed under its coverlet and cushions. Her raised eyebrows dismissed my home, and me, as ludicrously inadequate.

'I'm afraid Charles isn't here,' I said. 'Perhaps you'd care to leave a message for him . . .'

'We'll wait,' said Julian.

'We were just as anxious to make your acquaintance as to see Charles,' said Bianca,

63

whom I was beginning to dislike intensely. An enormous diamond solitaire glinted on her left hand, and on her right wrist she had an exclusively designed bracelet which screamed 'Cartier' at me. The pair of them moved in a smooth aura of money. At the back of my mind I had always known that Charles did, too, but when he was with me the difference in our life styles had not worried me. Now it began to do so.

'Perhaps you can settle a little argument for us,' said Bianca. 'Did Charles tell you about his fiancée or not? I thought he wouldn't have done so, but my husband is quite sure he would have done.'

'I'm sorry,' I said, which was quite idiotic of me. If I could have just dropped down in a faint, it would have been the perfect way to end a horrible conversation, but I wasn't the fainting type, and no matter how much I wished the Brenners elsewhere, they weren't going to budge on my say so.

'He didn't?' Bianca laughed. She should have practised laughing in front of a mirror. She had prominent eye teeth, and they became exposed when she laughed. 'Oh, my poor Sue! That is what he calls you, isn't it? Sue? Delightful name. He is a naughty boy, our Charles. But surely you must have guessed that he was a bit of a rogue where the girls are concerned? Why, he even had a go at me one night when Julian was out . . . but that's all to be forgiven now he's working with us.'

'Is he?' I asked. I wanted to sit down, but knew that I wouldn't make it to the nearest chair.

'Of course, my dear. Oh, you're thinking of his little naughtiness over the fraud case? Well, of course that was very bad, but when you remember that Charles' one ambition in life was to be a millionaire before he was forty . . .'

'Don't you know any other adjective but "naughty"?' I asked, and was ignored.

'I expect he'll give you a nice present for helping him out this week,' said Bianca soothingly. 'I'll say that for Charles, he always pays his way.'

'I do?' said Charles, speaking from the doorway. He was holding a bottle of wine in one hand, and his keys in the other. I hardly recognised him; his features might have been carved from soapstone, they looked so hard. This was a Charles I'd never met; the Double First who moved in moneyed circles, had a job in a Merchant Bank, and held his own with a millionaire reputed to be a bastard in his personal life. I ought to have guessed at his existence, but I hadn't, for up till now Charles had only shown me his warm-hearted side.

He turned to me, his eyes checking to see what damage had been inflicted in his absence. I don't suppose my face reassured him. He set down the bottle of wine, and shrugged off his coat. Neither of the Brenners moved. Both continued to smile.

'To what do we owe the honour of this visit?' asked Charles, his voice as cold as his manner.

'Visiting the sick,' replied Julian. 'How are you getting on, dear boy?'

'I told you on the phone. I'm flying out to join him tomorrow, and I don't know exactly when we'll be back. Maybe a week, maybe two. But I'll keep in touch, as I said I would.'

'But the money. You've missed a payment . . .'

'That was your fault, wasn't it? You shouldn't have put me in hospital.'

'You shouldn't have been so obstinate,' said Julian, but he didn't sound annoyed. He sounded quite pleased with himself. I didn't like the way his eyes continued to assess me while he spoke to Charles.

'I think we've seen enough,' said Bianca, rising to her feet in one supple movement. Her hips couldn't have been more than 34 inches; I didn't like to remember what mine measured. 'Don't you think so, Julian? She's not at all what I expected, but she'll do very well.'

'Agreed.' Julian got up, and held the door open for his wife. As she passed by, she picked up one of Charles' sweaters, which had been lying on the table, and thrust it at me. I recoiled, and the sweater fell to the floor between us. She laughed.

'Has he hurt her feelings, then?' she said. I couldn't look at Charles, or at her. I just stood there, waiting for her to hit me again. That was what it felt like; a series of punches to the solar plexus.

'There are limits to my patience,' said Charles, in that well-modulated cocktail-time voice of his. 'As you very well know.'

'Did we spoil something between you and Sue?' enquired Bianca. 'So sorry, darling!'

The door shut behind them. I heard Charles speak, but couldn't make sense of what he was saying. I thought I'd better see what had happened to my mayonnaise. It had probably curdled.

Charles whirled me round and shook me. This time I did hear what he was saying, he was asking how long the Brenners had been there, and what they'd said. I stared at him. I'd forgotten in this past week to think of him as a handsome man; I'd only thought of him as 'my' man, to be petted and fattened up and confided in, and loved. I'd forgotten perhaps deliberately my original suspicion that he must have a permanent girlfriend somewhere, and I'd managed to quiet my notion that he was being blackmailed. Now when I looked at him I saw a handsome stranger who was also a remarkably good liar.

'Supper won't be long,' I said. 'Why don't you go and pack? I think I'll scrap the Russian eggs, though. The mayonnaise won't come right.'

He reached for me. I stepped back, away into the kitchen, and closed the door. He didn't follow.

The rest of the supper seemed to be cooking to perfection. I jettisoned the curdled mayonnaise, and started to dish up. When I went back to lay the table, he'd gone. When supper was ready, I went through to tell him. He had just finished packing. By that time my pride had instructed me how to act. I would show him I didn't care about his other women, and that he meant as little to me as I did to him.

'You didn't tell me you were engaged to be married,' I said breezily. 'We must drink to your fiancée. Does she live in London?'

I expected him to look guilty, but he didn't. He half-smiled, smothered it, and followed me through to my flat without trying to touch me.

'So that's what Bianca told you? I'm sorry; I ought to have warned you about her, but I hoped you need never meet. I'm not engaged. I was once for three weeks, but when Dad was arrested she told me she thought we ought to postpone the wedding for a while. I did the noble thing and offered to release her from our engagement. She said " no, no!", but she didn't mean it. So I had a chat with her father and said we'd better just forget the whole thing. She was a nice girl, but she didn't have

68

the guts to last the course. Anything else you want to know about her?'

I took a mouthful of chicken and chewed. I shook my head. Charles sat opposite me as if we were strangers in a restaurant. Usually I laid his place side by side with mine, but tonight I'd put him on the far side of the table.

'Ronald didn't like her,' he said. 'He said I needed an emotional anchor, not a pennant to fly whichever way the wind might happen to blow. Felicity could never do what you have done for me. I can't imagine her ever offering me the comfort of her body, or . . .'

'You might have told me. It would have been more open.'

'I didn't want to tell you anything, you know that. Not until this is all over.'

'But why?' I pushed my plate aside. 'Bianca said you were a bit of a rogue where the girls are concerned. She also said you made a pass at her once.'

That ruffled him. 'I do not make a habit of hopping in and out of girls' beds, Sue. It's happened once or twice—yes. I was always ashamed of myself afterwards, because it didn't mean anything. As for Bianca . . .' He checked my face to see if I would take it. 'She made a pass at me, not I at her. And I had to decline the offer. That's partly why she hates me.'

His eyes slid away from mine, and I could see he was nerving himself to hear me call him a liar again. I didn't. Strangely enough, I believed him.

'All right. I accept that. But she said you were "naughty" over the fraud case, and I know they're blackmailing you.'

'Yes, and on the other hand, no. I am allowing myself to be blackmailed, if you like, but for an excellent reason.'

'To get at J.B.'s money?'

He didn't like that. His face tightened up and went cold on me.

'Well—what other reason can there be?' I asked despairingly.

'To get Dad out of jail, of course.' He said it as if it were the most obvious thing in the world. 'Don't you understand, Sue? He was framed for the fraud case, and the brains behind the frame have just been to see you, to make sure nothing will go wrong with their next job. This time I'm being set up as scapegoat. This time the stakes are higher; before, they played for forty thousand and my father's firm. This time they are playing for J.B.'s money and his life. They want me to murder him and arrange it so that Julian will inherit.'

I started to cry, partly from shock, partly from relief. I knew I was hearing the truth now. We abandoned the hardly-tasted meal and opened the wine. I needed it, even if Charles didn't.

The roots of the trouble lay in the past, in

John Brenner's marriage to a difficult woman who brought him money but no kindness or understanding. Their only child Julian was conceived in a desperate attempt to put some warmth into the marriage. He was born in the same month, and in the same nursing home as Charles, but his mother indoctrinated him from birth with the idea that his parentage entitled him to an easy ride through life. John Brenner was frequently away on business; there were rumours that he kept a mistress, but if this were true, he was discreet about it. Whatever the cause, his wife came to look on him simply as a source of money, and Julian copied her.

It was perhaps unfortunate that Charles was always around to act as foil to Julian, for Charles had been born with a quick brain, a thirst for knowledge and a dogged temperament that earned him every prize he cared to compete for at school, and brought him scholarships as he grew older. Charles was conscious of his ability, but not conceited, for his father and brothers—all men of steady character—banged it into him that though he had been born with a gift, it would do him no good unless he exploited it, and that that meant hard work. Luckily, Charles liked work. Julian didn't. Even if John Brenner had not had Charles constantly in sight, he must have been disappointed in his only son, for though Julian had been born with some brains, he had no inclination to use them.

When Charles was ten, John Brenner offered to pay his fees to a well-known public school. The offer was refused. Oliver Ashton said that Charles could either pay his own way, or go to the local grammar school as his brothers had done. In due course Charles won a scholarship to the same public school to which Julian had been sent. At that time they tolerated each other. Julian floated around at the bottom of the classes, making the least possible effort to get through school, waiting for the day when he could take up his rightful position in the world as a millionaire's heir. Charles found competition sharpened his mind and finished school with an armful of trophies to his credit before going on to Oxford on another scholarship.

After school Julian drifted from one thing to another, taking nothing seriously. His father found him jobs; he would keep them for a while and then, growing bored, would take off for the South of France or the Bahamas for an extended holiday before drifting back to Whitestones to ask for more money.

Charles enjoyed himself at Oxford. He revelled in setting himself impossible tasks and then completing them within time limits set by himself. He had one secret which he kept even from his family; every year on his birthday John Brenner wrote to Charles and offered him a job, and every year Charles refused, saying he wished to make his own way in the world. Charles spoke of this to no one, least of all to Julian, and yet when the two met, discomfort ruled. Charles came to the conclusion that Julian had discovered his father's offers of work, and resented them. He did not blame Julian for resenting them, but he did begin to feel sorry for John Brenner, and after he qualified and began to work for the Merchant Bank, he used to ask the millionaire to dine with him when he was in London. John Brenner aways accepted these invitations.

It seemed to me that the two men, the one old and powerful, and the other young but conscious of latent power, recognised each other's quality and were drawn to each other despite the difference in their ages and Charles' pride.

When Julian's mother died, he inherited a lump sum of money and married Bianca, who had as great a talent for spending it as he did himself. They bought a big mock-Tudor house in an expensive suburb of town and Julian played the Stock Market—disastrously. He got into debt. His father bailed him out and, discovering that most of Julian's money had gone this way and that, suggested his son might try accountancy as a last resort, under Oliver Ashton's eye. Julian refused. He plunged into some slightly questionable property deal which was to retrieve his financial position, it fell through, and he was left worse off than before. Once more John Brenner rescued him, and repeated the suggestion of a job with Oliver Ashton. This time he reinforced his suggestion by telling Julian that he had no wish to leave his money to someone who did not know how to handle it. He said that he had altered his Will, which had previously made Julian residuary legatee, subject to certain bequests to servants. The new Will left Julian a mere two thousand pounds per annum, with the remainder going to charity. John Brenner informed his son that if he could make a success of the job with Oliver Ashton, and show signs of settling down, he would tear up the new Will, and reinstate Julian as his heir. Julian had no choice but to take the job, but it rankled.

At first John Brenner's plan had appeared to work well. Oliver Ashton, working part-time since his operation for lung cancer a couple of years back, never believed evil of anyone if he could help it, and thought of Julian as a wayward child in need of kindness. He handed Julian over to a man called Robert Maudsley, who had been with the firm for years. Ronald Ashton, the second son, disliked Julian's presence in the office because he thought he did his work badly, but he made no complaint, since he did not wish to upset his father.

It was easy, afterwards, to see how the frame had been worked.

In Bianca, Julian had a wife with just as many brains as he, far more guts, and far fewer scruples. She and her husband worked on Robert Maudsley until he agreed to help them. Robert was a good choice; an ageing bachelor, he was qualified but had no capital, so that he could not set up by himself, and he had not quite enough brains to justify his being offered a partnership in the family firm. He had had an 'understanding' for years with Ruth James, who was Oliver Ashton's secretary, but had never 'named the day'. It was Robert who co-opted Ruth. Bianca provided the driving force and the brains, Julian and Robert the opportunity, and Ruth the necessary secretarial skills for the frame.

The first step was to select suitable clients; Oliver Ashton only worked half days, and the clients he didn't deal with were split almost equally between Ronald and Robert, with Julian sometimes helping out. The victims had to be people with money which they wished either to invest for the first time—such as a widow who had just received her husband's life insurance—or professional men who wished to take money out of stocks which were not doing well, so that it might be reinvested in a more profitable manner. Between them, Julian and Robert selected four such clients, and told them their problem would be referred to Mr. Oliver Ashton for solution. Needless to say, Oliver Ashton never even heard that they had any problem! The next step was for Ruth to write formal letters to each of these four clients, as if they came from Oliver Ashton, saying that he would be only too pleased to invest money on their behalf, if they would send him a cheque made out to him personally.

'Personally', that was the point. Usually such cheques would be made out to the firm, but in the letters which Ruth typed and signed on his behalf, it was clearly stated that the cheques were to be made out to Oliver Ashton in person. The police found this a most damning point, when they came to investigate.

When the victims sent in their cheques, Ruth intercepted them, put the letters in the appropriate files, and gave the cheques to her fellow conspirators. By that time either Robert or Julian—probably Julian, since he was most like Oliver Ashton in build—had got himself up in a white wig and opened an account in the name of Oliver Ashton in a bank in a neighbouring town. The manager of the bank knew Oliver Ashton by repute but not by sight; he was cynically amused when his new client explained that he wished to keep this second account a secret from his family. He asked, for instance, that his bank statements should be sent to his office. The fake 'Oliver Ashton' managed to convey that he wanted to run a second account in a different town in order to support a mistress there. The four cheques were paid into this secret account, and all but two thousand pounds were subsequently withdrawn by 'Oliver Ashton', in cash, over a period of about a month.

In time, of course, the four victims became restive. They wanted their share certificates, or at least some acknowledgement that their money had been received. One wrote, another phoned. Oliver Ashton couldn't understand what they were on about. One went to the police, and the Fraud Squad walked in. Perfectly timed, the bank statements for the secret account arrived at the office. Ruth handed them over to the police, in tears. Nearly forty thousand pounds had disappeared; two thousand had turned up in an account which had been opened by 'Oliver Ashton' under mysterious circumstances, and the letters from the clients were all on file, just as they ought to be. It was an open and shut case against Oliver Ashton.

Naturally Oliver Ashton denied everything. Then one evening Robert, Julian and Bianca cornered him with a handful of letters purporting to involve both Mary Ashton and Charles in the fraud. They were forgeries, but good ones; it turned out that Ruth had quite a talent in that direction. Oliver Ashton, frail and badly shaken by the case, couldn't stand the thought of his darling wife, and the son of whom he had been so proud standing in the dock with him. Broken, he bought their immunity; he sold the firm to Robert Maudsley and agreed to plead guilty to fraud, provided the incriminating letters were destroyed. Robert had an agreement ready to sign, together with a cheque for twenty thousand pounds. Julian and Bianca witnessed the sale, and then drove Oliver down to the police station and waited for him while he made a statement confessing his guilt.

Charles was in Paris on business at the time, and he had Felicity and his own future to think about, but he threw all that up to tear back home to see what he could salvage from the wreck. He was too late; his father could fight no longer. He had turned into a tired old man overnight. The police had their confession, and Ronald had already been dismissed from the firm he had always supposed he would inherit, and was without a job or prospect of landing one. Oliver told his sons to think of themselves, and not to waste time and energy on fighting the inevitable. Charles raged, to no avail. He and Ronald worked out how the fraud must have been committed. They ferreted out the weak points in the prosecution case; that the manager of the bank could not truthfully say that the real Oliver Ashton had opened the secret account with him, and that thirty-eight thousand pounds had vanished into thin air. David, the elder brother, wrote from Ireland to suggest that Charles pounded the truth out of Ruth, but that would only have brought Charles into court himself on a charge of grievous bodily harm. Oliver Ashton insisted that he must plead guilty, and did so.

He was tried—a formality—and sentenced. Ronald took the twenty thousand pounds for which the family firm had been sold, and went to work for his mother at Collett Cosmetics. That at least had worked out well. He and his wife now lived at Green Gables and kept Mary Ashton sane. Charles broke his engagement to Felicity and went back to Paris fighting mad, but unable to see what he could do about it. Ruth married Robert Maudsley, and Bianca brought herself a diamond solitaire.

To do him credit, John Brenner refused to believe that his old friend was guilty. Julian was stupid enough to taunt his father with having been friendly with a crook, and when that had no effect, threw in a hint that Charles had been involved, too. John Brenner replied that if Charles had been involved, the fraud would have been carried out so cleverly that it would never have been detected! Jealous, Julian flared up. There had been a row to end all rows, and a great many things had been said which would have been better left unsaid. In consequence, John Brenner disinherited his son completely, which set Bianca plotting once more—this time not for the paltry sum of nineteen thousand pounds which was Julian and Bianca's share of the original loot, but for John Brenner's life.

As before they needed a scapegoat, and for various reasons—because he had offended Bianca, and because he had always been a favourite of John Brenner's—the conspirators' choice fell on Charles rather than on Ronald. Julian and Bianca visited him when he got back from Paris, and threatened him with publication of letters similar to those which had broken his father, unless he left his job and went to work for John Brenner on their behalf.

Apparently Charles conceived a counterplot even while they were detailing their plan for him to fleece John Brenner of a considerable sum of money each month. Charles was not frightened by their threats, although he pretended he was; in reality he was eager for the opportunity to work with them, so that he might collect evidence to clear his father. He asked for time to consider. They gave him a week, during which he threw up his job, and turned practically everything he owned into ready money. Then he went to John Brenner and asked him for a job.

I think it must have been the hardest thing he'd ever had to do in his life, for even while he told me about it he ground his teeth. At first John Brenner had refused to believe that Charles was serious, so Charles had to spin him some yarn about having dropped a packet on the Stock Exchange, and wishing to gain experience in J.B.'s employ so that he could recoup. He made it clear to his future boss that he would use any information that came his way, while working for J.B., to make money on the side. J.B. had laughed, angry and disillusioned with his favourite, and dared him to try. Perhaps, too, some of the poisonous hints Julian had dropped in his ear had been absorbed.

'He wanted to punish me for letting him down,' said Charles, starting to pace the room. 'He probed for my weak spots, and I've got plenty. He considered it a day well spent if he could make me slam out of the room to avoid losing my temper. He really did have me licking stamps and . . . I saw it did no good to take it quietly, so I started to hit back. We threw words at each other like hand grenades. He abused me till he learned I would give as good as I took. But he didn't give me notice, and I stuck it out somehow, until he saw that I really was the same person, even if I had come a cropper on the 'Change. I do have a feeling for the way money moves. I do have the sort of background, and the training to work for, and even with him. He began to trust me again, and then to test me out . . . and then to wonder if I meant to stay with him or to leave as suddenly as I'd come. He tried to get me to talk about my financial affairs, and the real reason why I'd gone to work for him, but at the time I couldn't . . .

'He began to fret because he felt he had no hold on me. He'd been so lonely; fighting with me was the best thing that had happened to him for years. Like you, he knows when I lie. He knew from the beginning that I hadn't really gone to him to learn how to make money, although he saw that I was short . . . He tried bribery; he offered me a directorship in one of his companies, a new car. He tried to give me things—a valuable picture I'd admired, clothes, and so on. I returned them all at first, but . . . not the watch he gave me at Christmas. You see, he'd given a beauty of a watch when I was twenty-one, and I'd had to sell it with the rest of my things. He noticed that at once. He gave me another at Christmas, and I couldn't even thank him for it!'

He clasped and unclasped the watch angrily, staring into space. I was beginning to wonder if John Brenner cared for Charles in the same way that Charles seemed to care for his boss.

He slid over that part of the story which covered his 'business' arrangement with Julian and Bianca, only assuring me that although he had managed to satisfy them, he had not cheated his employer while doing so. The flicker of his eyelids and a half smile told me he would lie if I pressed him on the subject.

He wasn't sure whether Bianca and Julian had intended to murder J.B. from the start, or whether that idea had grown with the success of their scheme to plant Charles in J.B.'s household. However it had been, Charles had been completely unprepared for the use of violence.

The Friday night on which he disappeared was one of those on which he had been scheduled to meet the Brenners and Maudsleys to discuss the progress of their scheme. He was asked to stay at the Brenners for the weekend, because they had something important to discuss with him. Having agreed to collaborate with them, Charles had to agree to that, too. He collected his overnight bag from the boarding-house and turned up at the Brenners in time for supper. It was his custom at that time to have a sandwich for lunch, and he had been healthily hungry when he arrived. Over pre-supper drinks it was suggested to him that he put a forged Will into J.B.'s safe—a Will which would reinstate Julian as heir—and then tamper with J.B.'s insulin bottles so that J.B. would go into a coma and die. Bianca's idea was that Charles should put the Will into the safe on the following Tuesday morning, just before J.B. left on his trip south, so that he would be taken ill on the yacht, when it would be difficult to raise medical assistance quickly.

Charles raised a number of objections, which were squashed by Bianca. Finally he had to say 'no'. There was no explosion from Bianca. She suggested that he think it over while they had supper, and asked if he'd like to wash up first. She showed him into a bedroom which might once have been a nursery, for it had bars on the window. She locked the door and left him there. There were no sheets or blankets on the bed, the room was unheated, he had no coat with him—and he was hungry. There was a washbasin, so he had water to drink, and there was a pot under the bed. They left him there until Monday night, hoping that hunger and cold would persuade him where words had not.

Charles said that he could have broken out, but had decided against it. He had agreed to work with the conspirators, hoping for an opportunity to collect evidence which would free his father, and at the same time protect J.B. from harm. If he broke out, he would blow his cover and lose the only advantage he had. He sweated it out, his greatest fear that if he told the villains to go to hell, they might tamper with the insulin bottles themselves, while he was not there to warn J.B. So he sat it out.

When they came to fetch him on Monday evening, he was weak, but still active enough to give Julian a black eye, and Robert a crack on the knee.

Charles didn't detail what they had done to him. He said that at first their idea was not to damage him so that it would show, but that as time went on and he remained obdurate, they grew careless, and more inventive. He said he'd heard the clock chime ten and twelve but couldn't remember it striking eleven. Once they had to pour whisky down him to bring him round. Almost immediately after he lost consciousness again, and only woke up in hospital.

'And now they know about you,' he said, giving me one of his loving, anxious looks. 'Bianca saw that you were no one-night stand. She knows I'm serious about you, and that she now has the perfect weapon to make me do whatever she wishes. She only has to threaten to harm you, and I'll do as she wishes.'

'You wouldn't kill . . . !'

'Of course not. But I must join J.B. as quickly as I can, and keep him out of the country until we're ready to move. I mustn't see you again, until this is all over.'

'How long will it be, and what is it you are planning?'

'I mustn't tell you. I daren't. But it won't be long now. The next move is up to Ronald, and when he's got his bit of the jigsaw in place, I'll come back and tell Bianca that I'm willing to see sense—and that I'll do whatever it is that she wishes me to do. Darling Sue forgive me for dragging you into this?'

I was more frightened now than I had been before. I clung to him, and he to me. Presently we moved to the bed and made love slowly, sadly, for the last time.

I woke in the night, and waking, I roused him, too. I had taken to leaving the gas fire on at nights, partly because the weather had turned cold, and partly for company. I had no need to worry about bills, for as Bianca had hinted, Charles had been more than generous to me. It was warm, lying in his arms. The following night I would be alone and cold.

'I've been thinking,' he said, low in my ear. 'Every day this last week I've been able to tell myself that, incredibly, I was happy. Not just content, but properly happy.'

There were a lot of things that I wanted to say to him, such as that I was a stodgy Old Maid in the making, and that I didn't really expect to hear from him again once he'd gone, but I thought they might sound as if I were asking for promises from him, so I said nothing at all.

'Sweet Sue,' he said. 'When I was right down, wondering if I'd ever have the courage to face them again, along you came and said "I'm Sue", all soft and loving. I've been hanging on to you with my fingernails. I've never known what it was all about before. It explains so much; why Dad wouldn't allow

Mother to be drawn into it, and why David made Inge stop having children after she'd borne him three girls in three years. It even explains why Jane looks at Ronald as if she's going to cry . . . I've always felt the cold so much, till now.'

There was a heavy fall of snow in the night. He cleaned it off my car for me before he went.

FOUR

I lost nearly half a stone in the fortnight that followed. I don't quite know why; it just rolled off me. Bessie told me I was a fool if I thought I'd see Charles again, but even she was impressed by the six dozen red roses he sent me. I had to borrow a couple of vases from Rita in order to get them all into water. Charles never did anything by halves.

After some thought I told Bessie most of what Charles had told me. At first she refused to take me seriously, but later she said I ought to go to the police. However, when I pointed out that I had no proof, she agreed with me that we'd just have to wait and see what happened. I felt better when she knew about it. I didn't want to reason why, but even then I must have been aware that I would need some insurance to get through the adventure in one piece.

I bought some new clothes, and some wool so that I could knit Charles a sweater. I didn't go out at night much, because Charles usually phoned me between six and eight. He had found J.B. bursting with irritability at the stupidity of everyone around him, and had hardly allowed Charles to change into lighter clothes before setting him to work. Anyone might have overheard those telephone conversations. Charles would tell me the latest anecdote of J.B., and in turn I would tell him what I'd been doing. It was all highly satisfactory.

Then on the Thursday morning the postman left me a letter from Ronald Ashton, asking me to join him and his mother for a coffee in the Turkish room of the biggest store in town that evening, at six o'clock. On Thursday nights several of the big shops stayed open until eight at night.

I told Bessie about it, and she said ' What a giggle!' and that she might just be doing a spot of shopping herself that evening. Frown as I might, she was so curious to catch a glimpse of the Ashtons that she came into town with me, and only left my side when I entered the coffee bar.

I saw them before they saw me. At first I thought Ronald could have passed for Charles' twin, although he was a good stone heavier. Then I saw that Ronald's hair was a couple of shades darker and more conservatively cut. Ronald wore glasses all the time, whereas Charles only wore them for reading and driving. Ronald was dressed entirely in grey, he looked reliable and unassertive. He had commandeered a corner table and placed his mother with her back to the wall so that she had a view of whoever might enter. She was slim; her shoulders were tense beneath a simple jersey suit from Switzerland. She reminded me of a picture of Mrs. Siddons as the Tragic Muse, for she had the same carefully arranged dark hair and beautifully made-up face. Only eyes and mouth hinted at the anguish she was trying to suppress. A superb tweed coat was flung over the back of her chair, and rings glinted on thin fingers.

'Hello,' I said, with my hands deep in my pockets. 'I'm Sue Stephens.'

Mrs. Ashton surveyed me with all the enthusiasm of one presented with an untrained puppy. 'This . . . is . . . Susan?' she asked her son. Her fine eyebrows indicated that 'Susan' did not match up to expectations.

Ronald didn't even blink. He rose, handing me to a chair from which he had to remove a substantial briefcase. He looked me over thoroughly, without prejudice, and then smiled. I didn't think he normally smiled much; he wasn't that kind. He was a very serious young man.

'Delighted,' he said, sounding as if he meant it. 'Coffee or tea?'

'Black coffee,' I said faintly. 'Please.'

'I give up!' announced Mrs. Ashton, veiling beautiful eyes with blue-veined lids. 'I thought Charles at least, of all of you, might choose someone to do the family credit.'

'Charles knows what's good for him,' said Ronald, disposing of that topic of conversation. A waitress materialised in response to a flick of his fingers. I thought Ronald had all the virtues; fancy being able to summon a waitress in the busiest coffee bar in town, just like that! Ronald wore a wedding-ring; I wondered if Charles would wear one if he decided to get married. I thought he probably wouldn't.

'You are ready to move now?' I asked, feeling slightly unreal. 'Charles didn't say anything about it last night when he phoned me.'

'Right up to early this morning he was hoping he could keep Uncle John away until everything was ready,' explained Ronald. 'But Uncle John has to make a speech in Birmingham on Saturday night, and he won't even consider cancelling it. They are flying back this evening, and will spend the night in a hotel in London. Charles apologises, but he won't be able to ring you tonight. Tomorrow he and J.B. will be busy in London, and with any luck Charles will be able to persuade J.B.

to go straight to Birmingham on Saturday. That way he should be safe until Sunday, when we will be ready to move. Did you bring my note with you?'

I handed it over. He shredded it up, together with the envelope, and burned the remains in an ashtray. He was very thorough.

'Charles has told Uncle John what's going on, but Uncle John refuses to believe that his son really means to go through with it. He thinks that when it comes to the crunch, Julian's nerve will fail him. He believes that Bianca is the brains behind all this, and if he can only split the marriage up, he may be able to salvage Julian. It's possible. I'm not happy about it, but it is possible.'

'You're taking a risk,' I ventured. 'Couldn't you just tell the police . . .'

'What would we tell them?' he asked soberly. 'There's no proof. No, we have to let them incriminate themselves, while taking every precaution we can think of to safeguard Uncle John. I'm doing my bit tonight, and if the worst comes to the worst, we could move after that, although we'd prefer a couple more days grace.'

'Can I help?'

'Yes. Charles wants you to go away for the weekend—at our expense, of course. He wants you safely out of the way when we move.'

I shivered. My coffee came, and I drank it,

without sugar. I thought of pleading with him to let me stay and help, and then thought I'd better not.

'I'll go home for the weekend,' I said. 'I usually go once a month anyway. No need for a sub.'

They nodded approval. Mrs. Ashton's eyebrows still indicated that she found my appearance disappointing. 'Do you have to wear glasses all the time?' she asked.

'Yes, I do.' Her eyebrows now told me that she deplored not only the information, but the argumentative tone in which it had been given. 'Sorry!' I said. 'But that's the way I am. Now don't let's get worked up about this. Charles and I had a great week together, but we might find we haven't anything to say to each other when we meet again.'

Mrs. Ashton sighed. Ronald gave me a kindly, but reproving shake of his head. 'Charles has told us he intends to marry you,' he said.

'Oh!' I blinked with shock. 'But he's an awful liar, isn't he?'

Ronald looked shocked, but Mrs. Ashton viewed me with something that might have been approval. 'Very good, Susan. Perhaps you will be able to control him, after all. God knows, nobody else can.'

'Except Uncle John,' frowned Ronald.

'Oh, him!' She managed a smile. 'I almost pity Charles, working with John. His temper has been something diabolical these last few years.'

There didn't seem anything else to say. Ronald collected the bill and we rose to go. As we moved to the entrance of the coffee bar, the harsher light picked out a dozen lines on Mrs. Ashton's face which had been softened in the kinder glow inside. She looked ravaged.

Impulsively I touched her arm. 'I'm so sorry,' I said.

She stared at me full-eyed. Her composure was paper-thin. I took my hand away. Her pride was as high as her son's. Ronald shook me by the hand, a gesture kindly meant and gratefully acccepted. I saw there were many differences between the brothers. Charles was mercurial whereas Ronald was solid. Charles' eyes were never still, always observing and assessing; Ronald looked you full in the eyes and hid nothing. I liked Ronald, but I loved Charles.

Bessie caught up with me as Mrs. Ashton and Ronald disappeared into the crowd.

'Smashing outfit!' was Bessie's verdict. 'But doesn't she look sour!'

As we followed the Ashtons out, I told her, loftily that she didn't understand. Of course Bessie had to be brought up to date. She thought me feeble-minded, meekly agreeing to go away for the weekend while the Ashtons put their plan into operation. If she had been in my place, Bessie said, she would have forced Ronald to let her in on their secrets. I argued that the Ashtons knew what they were doing, and that as Bessie hadn't met Bianca, she couldn't appreciate just how nasty a piece of work she was. I said I was quite happy to leave the dirty work to someone else, so long as it didn't land Charles in prison, too, and . . .

'Come on!' hissed Bessie, grabbing me by the arm and hauling me after her out of the shop and across the street.

'What is it?'

'Ronald Ashton. I thought I saw him going down that alleyway over there. He looked over his shoulder to see if anyone was following him first. His mother must have gone on alone.'

'You're imagining things!' But I followed her. The alley connected the main shopping street with a quiet, tree-lined square of houses which were now taken over for use as offices. At a safe distance we watched Ronald—for it was he—cross the square, stand looking around him for a moment, and then disappear into a doorway. The square was very quiet; most of the office workers had gone home by now. Lights showed here and there in the houses, where the odd person worked late. A solitary street lamp lit the square. In a moment or two Ronald's figure appeared at a ground-floor window. We could identify him by the glare of the street light. He pulled down a blind, and a moment later the interior

94

of the office was illuminated as he switched on the lights inside.

'Burglary?' suggested Bessie, giggling.

'Nonsense,' I replied. 'I expect he's got every right to be there.' Nevertheless, I didn't exactly march across the square after Ronald, but tiptoed around the side. The house into which he had disappeared was an office, like the rest.

' "Robert Maudsley, Chartered Accountant" ', said Bessie, reading the plaque over my shoulder. 'It is burglary, you know, even if these are the offices his family used to own. He hasn't any right to be here, has he?' I fidgeted, not knowing what to say. I couldn't help remembering that Ronald had said he was going to ' do his bit ' that evening.

'We ought to ring the police,' said Bessie dubiously.

'How can we? He's Charles' brother, and we don't actually *know* that Ronald's doing anything illegal.'

'Watch it!' Bessie pulled me away as the light was switched off inside the office. Ronald's arm released the blind, and disappeared into the dimness of the room behind. Bessie and I scampered for the shelter of the nearest trees.

'No point in ringing the police now,' I whispered, as Ronald let himself out of the office and walked away across the square, his brief-case now under his arm.

'Now that he's got what he came for, you mean,' said Bessie. 'But if he has stolen something, what will happen when the police are called in? We can't just keep silent and pretend we didn't see him at it.'

'They probably won't find out about it till Monday, and by then maybe the whole thing will be over and it won't matter if we do tell the police.'

We watched Ronald out of sight, and then separated; Bessie to tell her boy-friend all about it, and I to ring my parents. Unfortunately I'd left it a bit late to ask if I might go home that weekend, since they had already accepted an invitation to eat out the following night. They suggested I had supper in my own flat, and then drove home to them afterwards. It seemed reasonable.

I can't say I did my work with an easy mind the next day. Bessie was unhappy about the situation, too, and made me promise that if the Ashtons did not tell me everything on Sunday night, I would go to the police. I agreed. I didn't want J.B.'s death on my conscience. After work I went back to the flat and started to cook myself some supper. I hoped Charles would ring me before I went home for the weekend. The very thought of seeing him again made me nervous. When the door-bell rang, against reason I was sure it was him, and flew to release the catch. A lighter step than Charles' came up the stairs, but I relaxed when I saw it was Bianca by herself.

'We must talk,' she said abruptly. She strode into my flat and looked around. Had she expected to see Charles as well? Then she swung back to me. 'You've lost weight. It suits you.' She didn't sound pleased about it. She was as immaculately turned out as ever. 'We have to do some entertaining this weekend,' she said. 'And I thought you could help us out with the cooking. I believe you're something of a dab hand with a wooden spoon.' She made my accomplishment sound contemptible.

'I don't understand,' I said. 'I'm not a professional cook, and anyway I'm due home this weekend. My parents are expecting me.'

'Then you'll have to cancel it. We have a bedroom waiting for you. Just pack a few things and come along without a fuss, there's a good girl.'

Now I understood. They had been making plans, too, and I had been elected hostage. If they held me, then Charles would be forced to do whatever they wanted. 'Don't try anything foolish,' she said, watching me. 'Julian is downstairs, and we happen to know that although Charles is back, he is going to be held up in a meeting for another hour.'

I glanced at my uneaten supper, and wondered what would happen to it. Then I measured her, and guessed that I carried more weight than she did, for all her height.

My suitcases were stacked one on top of the other above a big, old-fashioned wardrobe. I pulled the wardrobe doors open, and reached up for the bottom suitcase in the pile. The suitcases teetered. I tried, not too hard, to hold them back.

'Can you help me?' I asked. 'I think they're going to fall . . .'

She put up her arms to steady the top suitcases, and I pushed down on her shoulders, thrusting her forward into the depths of the wardrobe. Then I locked it, threw the key across the room, grabbed my coat and handbag, and ran. I took the stairs two at a time, and then, remembering Bianca had said that Julian was downstairs, peered through the coloured glass panel at the side of the front door. Sure enough, he was standing there, stamping his feet to keep them warm, with his big black overcoat pulled up to his ears. The lights of a passing car threw him into silhouette, and I identified him as the driver of Charles' car on the night of the 'accident'.

I rapped on Rita's door, and asked if she'd let me out through her french windows on to the lawn at the back of the house. I said someone had just called whom I didn't want to see. She was full of curiosity, but let me through. Down the garden path I ran, to the rickety gate in the fence at the bottom. Then through into the alley which served the back gardens of all the houses in our block. Ducking under the branches of an untended hedge in the dark, I was enfolded, arms and all, in the stifling harshness of a rug. I dropped my bag to fight it, but strong arms held me immobile. I kicked and heard someone wheeze and curse, but whoever it was didn't release me. Then something hit me on the head, and I felt myself daze and go limp. I woke half lying, half reclining on the muddy ground. My right arm was being pulled upwards. I fell on my back in the mud. Something hard and round was pressed into my chest. I tried to push it away but something round my wrists tugged them forward.

I focused my eyes in the beam of a powerful torch . . . the rug was on the ground beside me, and I was clasping a big shopping basket to my chest. My wrists had been bound round it and to its handles; the rope then went round my upper arms and was secured in the small of my back. Someone . . . a big, bold-featured man with dark, receding hair, was fiddling with my skirts. He bound a leather strap around my legs, just above the knees.

I opened my mouth to scream, even though the alley-way was deserted and the long gardens on either side would insulate the sound from anyone in the houses around. A wedge of cotton wool was thrust into my open mouth while someone got a grip on my hair from behind and jerked my head back. My eyes watered. I choked. I couldn't free my tongue. A scarf was tied tightly round my head, wedging my jaws open and the cotton wool well back over my tongue. A balaclava helmet was pulled over my head, leaving only my eyes visible. I was hauled to my feet. I nearly overbalanced, but the dark man steadied me.

Sobbing as if distraught, a strange woman picked up the rug, draped it round my shoulders and secured it in place with a safety pin. It fell nearly to the ground around me, hiding my bonds.

Still wheezing, the man began to push me down the alley away from the house. The woman picked up my handbag and ran ahead, delving into it. I tottered and fell, making animal noises, trying to thresh myself free. He didn't speak. He cuffed me over the head twice, deliberately, and then urged me forward with a boot at the back of my bound knees. I was crying myself when I stumbled, the very picture of a decrepit old lady, out on to the road which lay parallel to the one in which I lived. My own Mini was waiting for us, with the strange woman in the driving seat. My handbag was under the dashboard. The man pulled forward the passenger seat and pushed me into the back of my car, and as he did so, Julian and Bianca Brenner drove up behind us. The dark man gave them the thumbs-up sign, and we drove off in convoy.

I remembered Charles saying, 'It's only a very slight risk!'

The Brenners' house was large and well kept. Both cars were driven into a cavernous garage. I was hauled out, my legs were unstrapped, and I was propelled through a covered way into a well-designed kitchen and from there into a big living-room. By that time I was in a bad way. Bianca looked amused as she stripped off the balaclava helmet and scarf, and teased cotton wool from my mouth. Julian went straight to an enormous old French armoire in one corner of the room, and began pouring out drinks. Behind me a grandfather clock ticked, and chimed eight; the clock Charles had told me about, that he had heard chiming when he was being tortured in this very room. A wide oak staircase stretched up in front of me to a minstrel's gallery which gave access to the master bedroom and the guest wing. Architect-designed, the living-room was the focal point of the house. From floor to ceiling was nearer fifty feet than forty, and the illusion of height had been enhanced by the glitter of a chandelier suspended on chains from the oak-beams of the roof far above. A pair of giant settees flanked the fireplace, upholstered in chintz, a colour television set lurked in one corner, and the floor was smothered from wall to wall with a heavy white carpet.

'Robert here!' The dark man was at the telephone. He was wheezing still, and feeling in his pocket for an inhaler. 'We've got your girl, Charles. We expect to see you here in half an hour.' He didn't wait for a reply, but put the phone down. 'My allergy!' he complained. 'You ought to have let me cover the front of the house. You might have known she'd make a break for it.'

The other woman, who was presumably Mrs. Ruth Maudsley, still looked as if she felt like crying. She avoided my eye, fiddling with her hair.

'Come upstairs and get yourself cleaned up,' Bianca ordered me. She picked up a suitcase which I recognised as one of mine, and gestured me towards the stairs. I went up them, feeling like crying myself. Bianca didn't unbind my wrists or release me from the rug until I was safely in the bedroom the one with bars across the window. She watched while I rinsed out my mouth and tried to make myself presentable. It seemed to amuse her that my hands trembled.

'Was this really necessary?' I asked, when I could speak.

She didn't bother to reply. From her point of view, of course it was. She waited till I was ready, and then took me back downstairs. Robert and Ruth were already settled on either side of the fire, Robert inhaling to ease his asthma. Ruth's tweeds were expensive, but didn't fit well. Neither of them looked happy. Julian had changed; he looked as if he'd just stepped out of a window in Carnaby Street. Bianca curved her hand round a glass of whisky. Nobody offered me a drink, though I could have done with one.

'Why is he always late?' demanded Robert.

'Psychosmomatic,' said Julian. 'He likes to make a good entrance.'

There was a rush of tyres on gravel outside. A peremptory tattoo on the door knocker. Bianca let him in, and with Charles' coming, life stirred into the room. He stood as tall as Julian, but more solid; he'd put on more weight this past fortnight, and got some new clothes, a supple leather jacket and trousers. He was all in brown for once, even to the kid leather gloves he wore. He was tossing car keys in one hand. His eyes flicked over me without any noticeable change of expression and slid around the room, making an inventory of its contents.

'I'm in a hurry,' he said. 'J.B. wants me to rewrite his speech.'

'You know what we want,' said Bianca. 'Have a drink?'

'A ransom for Sue is that what you want? I might be able to manage another five, but . . .'

'The odd hundred or even thousand won't help you now, Charles. You know perfectly well what we want you to do.'

'No,' said Charles, and folded his lips hard.

'Tell him, Sue,' said Bianca, flicking at my cheek as she passed me on the way to collect a refill. 'Tell him exactly how we got you here.'

My throat was still too dry to make talking an easy matter, but I obliged. I tried to make the recital as matter-of-fact as possible. Charles' eyes were everywhere but on me while I spoke, and didn't return to me when I'd finished. He was wearing what I'd privately christened his 'stone face'. I couldn't guess what he was thinking.

'We didn't have to be quite so rough with her,' explained Bianca. 'But we thought a little show of force now might avoid a lot of trouble later on. And we have to consider poor dear Ruth's nerves, don't we? All that blood last time—it made you feel quite ill, didn't it, Ruth?'

'Yes,' said Ruth, in a stifled voice. She felt for her handkerchief again. Her husband said something to her in a vicious but low voice. She started to cry again.

'Well?' asked Bianca. 'Do we spreadeagle her over a chair and start on her with the carpet beater? Or shall we just tie her arms behind her back and throw her down the stairs once or twice, for starters? Tell me, Charles— did you suffer from nightmares this time as well? If falling out of a tree as a child gave you nightmares, surely being thrown backwards down the stairs here produced the same result?'

This time Charles did look at me, a spearing glance, gauging how much I could stand. I kept my head up and tried to stop shivering.

'All right,' he said. Everyone but me relaxed. 'Just what is it you want me to do?'

'You know perfectly well,' said Bianca. 'Substitute good for bad. Put the Will which we've prepared, and which Ruth has signed with a perfect imitation of J.B.'s signature, into the safe, in place of the Will which disinherited Julian. Then switch . . .'

'Wait a minute,' said Charles. 'Let's see this new Will first. Julian is sole heir, is that right?' Julian produced a manilla envelope from the armoire. Charles slid a Will form out of the envelope, glanced through it, and prodded it back before placing it in his pocket. 'I see. But you understand that I have to wait until he opens the safe himself? I don't have the combination—he doesn't trust me that far. He may open the safe tomorrow, to take out some cash for the Birmingham trip, but then again, he may not.'

'Then you must make some excuse to see that he does. Ask to check on something that's already in the safe. You are inventive; you can think of something.'

'Probably. But this business of switching the insulin bottle for one containing digitalin is another matter. I don't think you've thought it through properly.'

'He's on three injections a day, isn't he? The first thing you have to do is to make sure that he doesn't take his first injection one morning—or if he does take it, make sure it's pure water. That will ensure he'll really be in need of it by the time he broaches this lethal bottle. Then all you have to do is switch bottles so that the next injection he gives himself will be a lethal one.' Julian handed Charles a bottle with a flourish.

Charles pocketed the bottle. 'And how am I supposed to explain away his fatal heart attack?'

'Easy. You stage a quarrel with him. You could do it Sunday morning, as that seems to be the earliest opportunity you'll have, after putting the new Will in the safe. Then no one will be surprised when they find him dead—'

'With remains of a bottle containing digitalin beside him? That makes me suspect number one. I decline the position. If I go down, then so do you. Besides at Whitestones there are staff within earshot all the time; he'd only have to touch a bell to bring them running, get a doctor . . .'

'How about this?' suggested Bianca. 'Julian stages a reconciliation with his father, which will explain why J.B. has made a new Will reinstating his son as sole heir. Julian must get on the phone tonight to J.B., crawl to him, say he's sorry he's been such a naughty boy, that he wants to kiss and make up. He invites J.B.

to lunch on Sunday here. J.B. will accept, because he always does come round after quarrelling with Julian, doesn't he? Then while you're both here, you pick a quarrel with J.B. and storm out, leaving him reaching for his heart tablets and for his syringe. After he's given himself the fatal injection, we switch the bottles back again, and all the doctor will find when he gets here will be the rest of a perfectly ordinary bottle of insulin. That way nobody gets suspicious, and Julian inherits.'

'And I shall be in the clear? What about the cheques I've obtained for you?'

'Who's going to query them?' asked Julian. 'I shall inherit, and I'm certainly not going to query them, am I?

'And Sue?'

'Sue stays with us for the weekend,' snapped Bianca. 'She will be at liberty to move around the house, but not to leave. I hear she's a passable cook, so she can relieve me of that chore this weekend; in fact, she can cook us all a splendid Sunday lunch to celebrate Julian's reunion with his father. Robert and Ruth can come, too, to act as witnesses to the reconciliation.'

Charles was tossing his bunch of keys again. I wondered how his scars had healed. His eyes were on Julian. 'This is your father you're talking about. The man who sired you, and worried over you and rescued you from scrapes. You're not talking about a rat or a newly-born kitten; you're talking about putting down your own father!'

I thought Julian looked a little off-colour at that, but Bianca whipped in to prevent backsliding.

'This is the man who's disinherited his only son without adequate reason, who has neglected him for years, except to scold him. Yes, this is the man who broke his mother's heart and drove her to an early grave, the man everyone hates because he can't string two civil words together. Oh, he's an admirable creature! Well worth saving, isn't he, Julian?'

'Well?' asked Charles.

Julian made a defeated gesture. 'What I inherited from my mother—that's all gone now. I don't know how it went so quickly, but . . . then the money we shared out from the fraud case is nearly all gone, too. Dammit, I'm his only son; he owes it to me.'

Charles tried again. 'Why don't you ask for a reconciliation anyway? He'd clear you of debts, perhaps grant you an income from a Trust Fund. I'm sure he'd reinstate you in his Will of his own accord if you went to him and said you wanted to make up.'

'But I'd have to wait till he died to cash in, wouldn't I? And there'd be no guarantee that he'd not change his Will again. Besides, I'm all set to go through with it now. If we change our plans and then have to set it all up again at a later date, it might not be so easy to . . .'

'My strong-minded hero!' jeered Bianca, emptying her glass.

There was a solid silence. I could feel dislike and mistrust in the air, but no weakening of purpose. The Maudsleys had shrunk into onlookers.

'So you'll do it, Charles?' said Bianca softly. I wondered exactly how much it took to make her drunk. She was enjoying herself.

'Yes,' said Charles, and turned away to the door.

'Stop!' cried Bianca. 'The cheque—did you think I'd forget?'

Charles stopped, one pace from the door. 'What cheque?'

'The cheque you brought with you, of course. You mentioned money straight off, as soon as you got here, hoping to ransom Sue. So you've got a cheque with you, I'm sure of that. You've probably had it ready for days, against just such an eventuality. Slipped it in with a bunch J.B. was signing at the beginning of the month, perhaps? Let's have it.'

Charles reached into his breast pocket, produced a cheque and gave it to her. She held it up for us to see. It was signed by John Brenner, but otherwise blank. Neither date nor amount had been filled in.

'I do like dealing with Charles,' smiled Bianca. 'He twists and turns and thinks he's so clever, but he can't fool me, no matter how he tries. Fill it out for us, dear Charles! On the table here, so that we can all watch you. I do so love watching you commit a crime. It will be the last cheque, if we get rid of J.B. on Sunday, so make it out for a sizeable sum.'

I couldn't believe it. Charles had told me that any money he gave them was his own, and yet that cheque had been signed by John Brenner. I watched with shocked eyes as Charles filled in the date and completed the cheque in the amount of three thousand pounds.

'Generous!' commented Robert Maudsley, whose breathing was now back to normal. 'Why that makes it just over the sum we gave your father for the firm, doesn't it?'

'May I go now?' asked Charles, handing the cheque over.

'You may,' said Bianca graciously. 'But ring us in the morning to confirm you've put the Will in the safe and fixed the details for Sunday.'

'Oh the phone!' Once more Charles stopped by the door. 'I tried to ring you earlier on; there seems to be an intermittent fault on your line. I did report it, but . . .'

'Then send a telegram,' said Bianca. 'Early, though—we don't want to have to deprive Sue of food and drink, do we?'

Charles nodded. He was almost at the door. In a moment he would be gone. He had only looked at me twice all the time he'd been in the room. I couldn't bear it. I hadn't seen him for a fortnight, but the moment he'd walked in through the door that evening I'd known that whether he was being blackmailed, or was an out and out villain, I was in love with him. I called his name; I realised he didn't want to demonstrate any feeling for me in front of the others, but I couldn't let him go like that.

The next moment I was in his arms, and he was kissing me. I hadn't had much make-up on, and what I did have he took off in two or three shattering seconds. I was half off my feet, and short of breath when he swung me round with my back to the door, and whispered in my ear,

'Phone me at Whitestones when you can—day or night.' We changed positions, and he got busy on the other ear. 'We're almost ready—trust me!'

'I love you!' I said aloud, quite absurdly, for he must have known it all along.

'Yes!' he said, and hugged me so hard I thought it would be my turn for a couple of cracked ribs.

Then Bianca's face zoomed in, disagreeably close, and Charles' arms slackened and fell.

'What a crude technique,' she said in that barbed-wire voice of hers. 'Snatch and grab! No wonder Felicity opted out.'

'I must go,' said Charles, anxious eyes on me.

'I understand,' I said, trying to get it over not only that I had received his messages, but that I did believe in him.

'Yes, do go,' said Bianca, opening the front door for him. 'It's getting late, and Sue hasn't even started on supper for us.'

*   *   *

If I had been tired when the Brenners and Maudsleys had taken me from my flat, by the end of the evening I was exhausted. Neither Julian nor Bianca ate much, but both Ruth and Robert had done justice to my cooking. I ate the scraps they left over, and forced myself to clean the kitchen before going to bed.

It was an easy house to run; there was a hatch through from the kitchen into the dark-panelled dining-room, and a utility room on the other side of the kitchen, containing an enormous freezing cabinet now only half full of produce and a dishwasher. Somebody had spent a lot of money on the house. There was every labour-saving gadget you could think of, and when I had a chance to explore the house, I found the same evidence of wealth in every room. Julian's den, for instance, had its own television set and cocktail cabinet; it was a sad little room full of stale cigar smoke, with pornographic magazines tucked under the cushions of the biggest chair. Bianca's sitting-room was quite another matter; panelled in french grey, furnished in Louis Quinze style, brocaded and gilded, it looked more like a

112

show room in a West End furniture shop than a room in which you could relax.

I don't think Bianca did relax much except with the bottle. She caught Julian leering at me as I pulled on the banister to help myself up the stairs to bed. She nearly choked over her drink. 'Feel like trying her, Julian?' she asked. He went scarlet, and turned away to his den. She yelled after him that she was taking the bottle to bed with her in lieu of anything more potent. At that I turned my own head away, so that she should not see me blush for her or Julian.

Was his impotence at the root of her unhappiness? Or had she made him impotent by her attitude to him? either way, it was a most unhappy marriage. I thought of Charles telling me he'd always felt the cold until he slept with me, and knew he'd meant something even deeper; that he'd never had a satisfactory relationship with a woman until he'd met me. At that moment I pitied the Brenners.

'I'm not locking you into your room,' Bianca said, appearing in my doorway as I began to undress. 'The front and back doors are double-locked, but that's to stop burglars breaking in, not to prevent you leaving. You understand why, don't you?'

'I think so. If I don't play ball with you, then you'll leave the bottle of digitalin at the side of J.B.'s body on Sunday, so as to incriminate

113

Charles.'

'That's right, poppet. You behave yourself, and you can take the bottle of digitalin away with you on Sunday. And by the way, if Charles shows any signs of weakening before then, you might remind him that we've got enough on him already to send him to jail for a long time. You saw for yourself how he's been fiddling money out of his boss.'

I shook my head. She had a fine instinct, had Bianca. She knew that the affair of the cheque had upset me. Luckily I had the sense not to discuss it with her.

'Early morning tea at half past eight,' she ordered. 'And for God's sake don't make too much noise pulling back the curtains when you bring it in.'

I woke at seven, dressed rapidly, and after listening at all the bedroom doors to see if anyone else was awake, I went downstairs to phone Charles.

He was inclined to curse me for ringing so early. He said he'd been up till two rewriting J.B.'s speech, and that J.B. had got him out of bed again at four, because he'd had an attack of cramp.

'For heaven's sake—hasn't he got lots of servants . . . ?'

'He was jittery with nerves and wanted reassurance,' yawned Charles. 'He's not looking forward to Sunday any more than I am.'

'You told him—'

'Everything. Yes. You should have been privileged to listen in to Julian's phone call; it made me want to throw up. Hell, I'm still seeing Japanese Yen . . . you see, he'd made this point in his speech about investments in . . . Well, you wouldn't understand it, Sue, but I thought he'd got it wrong, and we had an argument about it. I should have let him carry his point, then I wouldn't have had to rewrite his speech, and I would have got an unbroken night's sleep for once . . .'

'You asked me to ring you,' I said, trying not to laugh. 'Now wake up, Charles! What is it you want?'

He cut himself off in the middle of another yawn. 'The phone! That's it! Thanks for reminding me. Now look—do you know anything about phones and how they work?'

'Don't be daft!'

'Well—this is what I want you to do . . .' He gave me precise instructions and made me repeat them.

'And that's all you want me to do?' I asked, disappointed. 'But I don't see how that will help . . .'

'It will. There's just one other thing you might be able to do, and that's find out where Bianca keeps her business papers; cheque book, bank statements, bills and so on. I should imagine they're somewhere in her sitting-room, and knowing her, that they're

115

kept locked up. Maybe a safe? Could you take a quick look round, if you have a chance . . . ?'

'And then ring you back?'

'No. We're off in an hour, and won't be back till after midnight, I dare say. Maybe someone will contact you . . .'

'But they can't, if I put the phone out of order.'

'Yes, well . . .' There was a confusion of noises in the background at his end of the phone, and then he came back to me. 'Just my breakfast arriving, and J.B. wanting to know who the hell I'm talking to at this hour of the morning. Look, could you sneak out to meet me early tomorrow morning, before breakfast? There's something I've got to ask you, and . . . I'll be at the end of the drive from half six on.'

'I'll try.'

The phone went dead. I didn't replace the receiver, but put it down on the table while I sought for a screw-driver. The kitchen drawer was well supplied. I unscrewed the casing of the telephone, depressed a wire with the screwdriver so as to break contact, and replaced the casing. I tested the phone and found it completely dead.

That worried me. I'd been asked to stop the phone ringing, but not told to break the connection entirely. I hesitated, not knowing what to do about it. I argued it was better to have the phone not working at all, than to put it to rights. Besides, I didn't know what it was I'd done wrong, and I wasn't sure I could repair the damage, even if I wanted to do so. I went to prepare breakfast.

Julian drifted downstairs at half-past nine, declaring he had a headache and couldn't possibly go into the office. Anyway, it was a Saturday, and he had never seen the point of working on a Saturday. I mixed him some salts.

Bianca didn't need salts. She must have acquired quite some tolerance to whisky, for she didn't even have a hangover when she got up. She went over the menus for the weekend with me, and made out a shopping list of the things I would need. I asked her to fetch my knitting from my flat as well, if she'd time.

'You've lost a little weight,' she said, eyeing me. 'But you're still no glamour piece. Charles won't stick to you, you know.'

'Charles isn't interested in glamour,' I said, and then knew I'd have done better to have maintained a discreet silence. I could feel violence in the room. Her fingers curled and uncurled, touched her throat, the buttons on her dress, a kitchen knife that lay nearby. Her tongue flicked over her lips. Her eyes never left me. I shivered and couldn't think of anything to say. I could feel that she wanted to hurt me, physically.

The door-bell rang. She didn't move.

'Shall I go?' I asked, stiff-tongued. 'It might

be the telegram you were expecting.'

She lowered her eyes and nodded dismissal. It was an effort for me to hold my back straight as I went to the front door.

It was a telegram. I handed it to her. She ripped it open and read it aloud. It confirmed that J.B. and Charles would arrive at noon on Sunday for lunch. It had been sent by Charles.

'What is it?' asked Julian, hand to head. Bianca passed the telegram to him, and told him to go out for a walk to clear his head.

'It doesn't say he's actually switched the Wills around,' objected Julian.

'How could he put that in a telegram?' asked Bianca, and for once I sympathised with her.

'The phone must still be out of order,' said Julian, testing it. 'Oh, hell.'

'A nice job for you,' said his wife. 'Just about up to your weight. You can go to the corner phone box and report it out of order.'

'But Charles said he reported it yesterday, and it must be a good mile . . .'

'. . . and don't take the car. The walk will do you good.'

I thought he'd object, but he didn't. That little exchange convinced me, as nothing else might have done, that Bianca wore the trousers in the Brenner household. Perhaps J.B. had been right in thinking that if he could only work on Julian, the plot against his life would collapse, but I didn't think he'd have

118

much chance to separate them. Bianca knew on which side her bread was buttered, and Julian seemed obsessed—no, fascinated—by his wife.

He put on his overcoat, and went out. I returned to the kitchen, hoping that Bianca would not follow me. Then the door-bell rang again. I set the kitchen door ajar, to see who it was.

'. . . it's really too bad,' Bianca was saying to someone at the front door. 'The fault was reported yesterday and you did nothing whatever about it . . .'

A man's voice mumbled something.

'I daresay!' said Bianca tartly. 'But what's it to me if your van has broken down and half the telephone engineers are off sick? We pay our rental and expect an efficient service.' She raised her voice. 'Sue! Come here!'

I took the grin off my face and went through. A middling-sized man in overalls too big for him stood in the doorway, holding a heavy bag of tools in one limp hand and blowing his nose with the other. His eyes were red, gingery hair stuck out in untidy clumps from under a floppy woollen cap, and he was a most unhealthy shade of greenish-white.

My first reaction was that Bianca might have been less hard on a man who ought to be in bed rather than attending to faulty phones. My second was to wonder how I was to explain to him about the damage I'd done to the phone.

'Sue!' said Bianca. 'This man has come about the phones. Don't let him stay here by himself and see he doesn't take anything away with him when he leaves.'

The engineer looked understandably depressed. He drifted across to the phone, and set down his bag.

'Very well, Mrs. Brenner,' I said, in best parlourmaid fashion. I could feel a giggle start at the back of my throat. The telephone engineer ought to have disguised his hands in mittens; they were too clean by half, squarecut and strong-looking. I watched him take the casing off the phone while Bianca checked she had everything she needed for her shopping trip. I had studied Charles' hands often. This man was smaller and older than Charles, but he'd been bred in the same stable, and the wig and make-up he wore hardly concealed a scar slashing across one eybrow. How blind Bianca must be not to see how beautifully controlled was his every movement! This was no pit-pony, but a finely-trained racehorse.

He coughed dismally and managed a sniff as Bianca let herself out of the house. He didn't seem disturbed by the damage I'd done to the telephone. Bianca's car snorted off down the drive.

'Coffee, David?' I asked.

FIVE

'Never take an unnecessary risk, Sue,' said David Ashton. 'Suppose Bianca had forgotten something and come back to the house for it? Or Julian had wandered in and heard you call me David? Now where's her papers?'

'Talk of unnecessary risks!' I said indignantly. 'What about you? What happens if Julian does walk in and find you burgling Bianca's desk?'

'In her desk, are they?' He took his bag and went off into Bianca's sitting-room. I hadn't had much time to look around between my spells in the kitchen, but it hadn't taken me long to find that one of the deep drawers of Bianca's desk had been lined with a metal container. The top opened upwards, in two halves, but was secured by a lock for which there was no trace of the key.

'Watch the door for me,' said David, fishing some probes from his bag. 'I need about half an hour clear in this room, without interruption.'

'Suppose Julian comes back? He's only gone for a short walk.'

'Then you'll tell him that the telephone engineer is tracing a wiring fault on the extension phone in here.'

'But if he recognises you . . .'

'Not got up like this, he won't. We've not

met for years, and anyway the Brenners of this world don't study the faces of their social inferiors. Now get out and make me that coffee you were talking about, will you?'

I made the coffee. When I took him in a mug, he had the box open and was replacing the bulb in the desk lamp with one of a stronger calibre. I opened my mouth to protest and closed it again. David Ashton knew exactly what he was doing. While I hovered in the doorway, he took photographs of certain papers which he'd selected from the drawer. Only when he'd finished and was locking them away again did I notice that he was now wearing cotton gloves.

'Tell me,' I said, 'Will you be present at the festive lunch tomorrow?'

'Of course not. I'm at present in bed with flu in Belfast, and likely to stay there for at least another day, or so Inge tells me. I think she'll probably have to call the doctor in tomorrow to check that I'm not going to die on her. I shall drop these negatives into Whitestones, change at Green Gables, and be on the next plane back to Belfast.' He replaced the ordinary bulb in the lamp and tidied the desk, checking that he'd left everything as he'd found it. 'It's worth a little risk. Oh, by the way, Sue Charles is looking very fine drawn. He can take a lot of pressure, but dealing with J.B. on top of everything else seems to me to be asking for it. Take him away for a holiday when this is finished, will you?'

'Everyone seems to have elected me Charles' keeper—except Charles himself. If he does want to marry me, then he might make an effort and put it into words!'

The front door clicked open, and Julian strode in, calling for his wife. David's carriage reduced to a slouch as he bent for his bag and I hastened to distract the master of the house.

'Telephone engineer,' I explained. 'Checking on that fault. Can I get you anything—some coffee?'

'Oh—perhaps.' He made as if to follow me to the kitchen, but stopped to pick up a newspaper. He unfolded it, intent on something.

'Aspirins for your headache?' I asked brightly. 'Did you take some?'

David crept out of Bianca's room and made his way behind Julian's back to the disembowelled telephone by the door. Julian gave him half a glance and returned to his paper.

'I don't think so,' he said absently. 'Just bring the coffee here, there's a good girl.'

'I don't like to think of you not taking aspirins if you've still got a headache,' I said, closing in on him, and trying to look worried. I expect I succeeded, for I really was worried. David screwed the casing back on to the telephone and tested it. Judging by the rigid

123

set of his shoulders and the way he set to dismantling it once more, the phone was still dead. I cursed myself yet again for my ham-handedness.

'You're an odd girl, aren't you?' said Julian, a little amused. 'I couldn't think what Charles saw in you at first, but I suppose some men like to be waited on hand and foot. Then again, if you're as sensible as you look, you'll pretend to be short-sighted if you spot lipstick on his handkerchief, or suspect he's been working late rather more than is necessary.'

'I don't think he's like that.'

'Don't say I didn't warn you. Your devotion may soothe his pride for the moment, but I daresay he'll be sniffing at Bianca's heels again within a month.'

'Do you really believe that?' I had almost forgotten David, working away in the background. I held Julian's eye with mine until his eyelids flickered and he looked away. No, he didn't really believe it.

'Coffee!' he said, to change the subject. He picked up his paper, sat down, and held it as a barrier between us. David tested the phone, and found it in working order. He gave me a thumbs-up sign, and made for the door.

'I'll just let the telephone engineer out,' I said to Julian's paper. He rustled it, but didn't reply. I wanted to ask David if his hair was really that bright ginger, but didn't dare. He mounted an old bicycle and wobbled off down the drive. Bianca didn't get back for another hour, but I was happy to see that she'd brought my knitting. With luck, I might be able to finish the back of Charles' sweater that day.

*   *   *

I stole down the drive at six next morning. It was still dark and sticky underfoot from rain which had fallen in the night. I clutched a Thermos of hot coffee and a packet of bacon sandwiches, and amused myself with romantic dreams of the way in which Charles would propose to me. I ought to have known better.

He'd parked under some trees near the road. He was huddled down in the driving seat, fast asleep, his driving glasses slightly askew on his nose and his hair ruffled. He woke as I relieved him of his glasses and the flask.

'A fine thing!' I scolded. 'How many more times am I going to come across you at the side of the road, dead to the world?'

'You're all right?' He smiled at me with some difficulty. I was shocked at his appearance, for he looked quite gaunt. He folded me in his arms, Thermos and all, and hid his face in my hair. His fingers quartered my face, to make sure everything was still in its right place.

'You're not to go back. I'll take you to

125

Green Gables, and Mother will look after you.'

'Nonsense. Have a sandwich and some coffee and you'll feel better. You know perfectly well that I've got to go back, or they'll get suspicious.'

He engulfed one sandwich and reached for another, showing signs of revival.

'Cupboard love!' I accused him.

He nodded. He hadn't shaved, and was wearing a dinner jacket under his overcoat. It didn't look to me as if he'd been to bed at all.

'Now what I wanted to ask you,' he said, obviously finding it difficult to concentrate, 'is whether you want to move into Green Gables today, just for the time being. Mother says it would be best; she wants us both under her eye. I'm not in favour of it myself, but I promised I'd ask you.'

I might have known I wasn't going to get a proper proposal of marriage.

'I don't think it would be a good idea,' I said, trying to get it across that his mother and I were not likely to live together in harmony.

'Neither do I. Then that's settled. I'll tell Mrs. Green—that's J.B.'s housekeeper, and she can stock up the larder for you. My flat at Whitestones is more than big enough for two. Now wait a minute! There was something . . . oh yes! The cooker is electric, and yours was gas, wasn't it? But you can cope with it for a couple of days, can't you till I can get you

126

fixed up with a gas cooker?'

He appeared to think that that disposed of all our problems. I opened my mouth to protest. I didn't know where to begin. I hadn't met J.B. yet, but I didn't like what I'd heard about him, and I was sure I didn't want to live in his pocket. Then again, I was damned if I was going to start married life in a furnished flat in someone else's house! By the time I'd sorted out a mild objection, Charles had fallen asleep against me, a half-eaten sandwich clutched in his hand. I guessed he was running a temperature, for his forehead burned against my cheek. David had said Charles was looking fine-drawn, but I thought that was an understatement; to my mind, he looked ill. I cradled him in my arms and let him sleep. It was early yet, and there would be time enough to sort out plans for the future after lunch. I had intended to ask Charles a lot of questions, but I decided those must wait, too. I knocked my knee against his car radio, and silently cursed it. I wondered at Charles for having kept a gift from the Brenners, after what they'd done to him. A surprising choice for a gift, too.

He woke slowly, just before eight. My arm had gone to sleep, and I had cramp in one leg.

'Two hours sleep is not enough,' I suggested. 'What's J.B. been up to?'

'Nothing. We got back late, but neither of us felt like sleep. We played chess for a while,

127

and there were one or two jobs I had to do . . . He started raking up the past, wondering if he'd acted differently in the past . . . whether it would have made any difference . . . he doesn't want to believe his only son is capable of . . . But he wants to go through with it. He has to be sure one way or the other.'

He looked around, dazedly. He'd chosen a quiet spot, just where the drive bent round into the road. You couldn't see the house from there, but a boarded-up potting shed nearby seemed to remind him that he was on Brenner property. He stared at it, and then down at his left hand, opening and shutting it. The skin was still seamed with scars, and always would be.

'You want me to leave J.B. when this is over,' he said, reading my mind. 'But it's not as easy as that. He wants me to stay. If I do go, he'll revert to being an invalid within months.'

'You're not an office boy. Surely you want to go back to London, to the sort of job you were trained for?'

He didn't seem to hear me. 'When he saw what they'd done to my hand, he cried!' He pressed both his hands to his forehead. 'I can't think straight about this, Sue. Of course I always intended to go back to London. Of course he's an unreasonable, selfish, tyrannical . . . only, in everything except blood, I'm his son. Can't you see that?'

I didn't want to. 'We'll discuss it later. We'll

128

go back to my flat tonight so that you can get a good night's sleep, and talk it over tomorrow when you're feeling better.'

He didn't say anything to that. I said I ought to be going. He grasped my wrist.

'Bianca—she's not harmed you? I've not had a moment's peace since I heard she'd got you. She's jealous, I'm sure. It's not safe for you to go back there . . .'

I shook my head, and got out of the car. He had been working for this for six months, and I wasn't going to upset his plans at the last minute. Besides, I wanted to be in on the showdown. I was to regret my decision, but at the time it seemed the right one.

'Go and get some sleep,' I said. 'I'll see you at noon.' He watched me out of sight.

*   *   *

I laid the dining-room table for seven; Julian was to be at the head with Ruth on his right, opposite Bianca who had placed John Brenner the guest of honour on her right, and Charles on her left. I was to sit between J.B. and Robert, across the table from Charles.

I cooked lunch automatically; turkey and all the trimmings, a salad, brussels and roast potatoes. There was a syllabub and a Stilton cheese to follow.

At five minutes to twelve Julian emerged from his den and handed Bianca a cutting

129

from one of the Sunday newspapers, reporting on financier John Brenner's speech the previous evening in Birmingham. Bianca was on her third whisky; both of them were dressed to kill. The Maudsleys arrived at three minutes to twelve. Both looked as if they'd slept badly, and Robert was at his inhaler. Neither of them seemed to fill out their clothes properly.

'Funny thing,' said Robert, accepting a glass of soda water with a splash of whisky in it, 'Man came in from the Fraud Squad yesterday morning and asked for me. I was busy with a client, so only had time to pop out and tell him he could look where he liked. Same story as before—checking on a complaint from a client who thinks he's been defrauded. Wish you'd been in, Julian—would have made it look better.'

'I had a headache!' said Julian petulantly.

Ruth coughed. 'I wished I'd still been working at the office when Robert told me about it. He thinks I'm just being fanciful, but I don't like to think of policemen poking into our files so long after . . .'

'Human nature,' said Bianca, her voice jagged as she helped herself to whisky without soda. 'I suppose some stupid old cow has just woken up to the fact that Oliver Ashton fiddled the books months ago, and is worried that he might have cheated her too. She loses her false teeth in fright, and tears straight off to the police without first checking that her money's safe.'

'I suppose so,' said Ruth. 'But you must admit it is odd. I told Robert to ring the Inspector in charge of the case and have a chat with him, but we couldn't get hold of him again yesterday.'

Nobody offered me a drink. I wandered over to the window which overlooked the drive.

'My father is always five minutes late,' said Julian, his voice itchy with irritation. 'Just like Charles.'

A silver-grey Rolls crept over the gravel drive and decanted a tall man with a thatch of hair the colour of dirty cream. He wore an expensive tan, and a silvery grey suit to match the Rolls, I suppose. His physique was similar to Julian's, in that he was also stork-thin and narrow-shouldered, but there the resemblance ended. Nose, chin and brows jutted forward above scrawny neck. His body inclined forward from his hips as he shot instructions at the chauffeur, his eyes restlessly scanning the drive. His fingers snapped, indicating nervous tension.

Charles' car swung into the drive and parked beside the Rolls. Charles had shaved and changed into his brown leather outfit, but I didn't think he'd slept since I saw him that morning. He still twirled keys, but had forgotten his gloves. The chauffeur drove off in the Rolls. Charles and J.B. spoke together for a moment. Much of a height, they were also on the same wavelength mentally; a sentence half begun by one was completed by the other, and a grimace was responded to with a shrug and a quick shake of the head.

'At last!' sighed Bianca, as Charles rang the door-bell. Then the newcomers were in the room, and J.B. was explaining that he'd sent the car back for some minor adjustment to the tuning, and that Charles would take him back to Whitestones later. Charles hung back, allowing J.B. to take the stage. J.B. greeted everyone in turn; an affectionate word for his son, a smile when he was complimented on the previous night's speech by Robert and then Bianca introduced me and I felt a wave of hostility emanate from him. His eyes tried to beat me down. He had very thin-lidded eyes, deeply set. He smiled at me, but it was a mere twitch of facial muscles, a social necessity, not intended to be taken seriously. I understood that he was jealous of me and my influence on Charles. I stared back at him, produced my sweetest and falsest smile and told him that I'd been longing to meet him.

Liar! his eyes said.

Charles slipped his arm under mine. 'Aren't you drinking, Sue?' I relaxed. J.B. glared at us both, and turned away. He knew now that if it came to a battle between us, I would take Charles away from him.

'Yes, we must all drink to our reunion,' said Bianca gaily.

'And to the happy couple,' added J.B., with a crocodile grin. 'I gather Charles is getting a licence on Monday. We ought to drink to Charles and Sue as well, don't you think?' I revised my first opinion of him. He had something up his sleeve, and it wasn't going to be a walk-over for me.

'The happy couple!' toasted Robert.

'Charles and Sue!' echoed J.B., sipping at a drink placed in his hand, and then putting it down as if he suspected it might have been poisoned.

'What are we all standing for?' asked Julian. 'Take the weight off your feet, father.'

'I might as well,' said J.B., sinking into a chair and passing one hand across his face as if washing it. 'Not feeling quite the thing today. Pity we've got that appointment at half three, or we could have taken our time over lunch, but as it is, I wonder if we might eat early—if it doesn't upset your arrangements too much . . .'

'Three o'clock,' said Charles. 'The appointment is at three, and at their place, not at Whitestones.'

J.B. stared at him. 'I told you . . .'

'They couldn't make any other time.'

The clash left reverberations in the air. Both men had strong personalities and both could be abrasive; both were now frowning. I

133

checked on the expressions worn by the Brenners and Maudsleys and found them all registering satisfaction.

'Shall I serve lunch now, then?' I asked Bianca. She nodded.

J.B. stood up, or tried to, and then sank back into his chair. His face registered anger. 'Cancel it! I will not have my orders set aside.'

Charles shrugged and asked if he might use the phone. I wondered if this little exchange had been a put-up job or not; I came to the conclusion that if I had to wonder about it, the others would be taking it for the real thing. I came to another conclusion. I liked J.B. about as little as he liked me, and that under no circumstances whatever would I live under the same roof as him, or allow Charles to go on working for him.

I put the food on the table while the others drifted in. Julian didn't look into his father's eyes when he spoke to him, but addressed a spot just below J.B.'s collar. As we sat down, Ruth made a brave attempt at sociability, complimenting J.B. on the gaily-patterned shirt and matching tie that he was wearing.

'A Christmas present,' said J.B. He didn't even glance at Charles, but I knew who had given them to him. Bianca started to carve; I thought it was typical of the Brenner household that she should undertake this fnction. Julian poured wine. Neither Charles nor J.B. wanted it.

J.B. yawned and tried to smother it. 'I'm glad you rang me, Julian—been thinking for some time that we ought to make up our quarrel—blood's thicker than water, and . . . anyway, I wanted to discuss this question of my Will with you. It wasn't altogether fair of me to disinherit you as I did. I was too hasty.' Having let off his firework, he lapsed into silence.

The conspirators exchanged glances. Charles stolidly helped himself to the salad. Bianca slashed at the turkey angrily. J.B. started washing his face again.

Charles leaned forward. 'Are you all right, sir?'

'Of course,' snapped J.B., removing his hand. 'Yes, a good opportunity, as I was saying . . . especially with Robert being here as well. Almost providential.'

'What changes were you thinking of, father?' asked Julian, his voice going high.

'With the coming of Old Age, one fears death more and not less,' said J.B., smiling. I could see it was all a party trick, and that he could lay charm on with a trowel, just as Charles could do. 'One begins to think of all the sins of commission and omission which one may have committed. One has more time for reflection, for reading, for thinking how little it matters if one doesn't always get one's own way.' I found his plea touching, even while my brain warned me it was calculated.

He filled his glass with water, and sipped at it, staring down the table at Julian. 'You are my only son, after all. In some sense you are what I have made you. Need I say more?'

'You mean,' said Bianca with care, 'that you are going to reinstate Julian as your heir?' I could see her brain struggling with the problem : ought they to call their plan off, and risk the old man changing his mind again—or carry on?

J.B. sighed. He was only playing with his food. 'I'm not sure that that would be a good thing, Bianca. Julian has done better than I expected since he started work for Oliver—for Robert here. The job seems to have provided him with a certain measure of stability. It may well be that a modest inheritance . . .'

'A modest inheritance!' Bianca's voice was strident. 'I thought you were talking of reinstating him as your heir!'

J.B. yawned again. He was speaking more and more slowly. 'Forgive me. I appear to be in need of another injection sooner than . . . I should explain that I have no intention of leaving all my money to Julian since he has neither the brains to administer the estate properly, nor the sense not to let you squander it for him. What I had in mind was to establish a Trust Fund in favour of my old college, so that they may build a Science Laboratory, bearing my name. Then there are various bequests to servants—annuities, and so on. I want to settle a sum on Julian sufficient to bring him in an income of two thousand pounds a year, and to buy him a partnership in Oliver's old firm . . . that is, if Robert here agrees.'

Everyone stopped eating, except Charles. Bianca's eyes were wild. She fixed them on her husband, who was looking at his father with the sick, intense glare of a trapped animal. His chin trembled.

J.B. dabbed at his lips. 'What do you think of the idea, Robert? I thought you might appreciate some extra capital, and if Julian puts in only a minimum of work . . . it would have to be a proper partnership agreement of course, with Julian getting his due share of the . . .'

'What about me?' demanded Bianca. 'What becomes of me under such an agreement? Two thousand a year, and slaving at that second-rate firm? We could hardly keep this house going and . . . my dress bills alone . . .'

'No one asked your opinion,' said J.B. His hands trembled. He stilled them by laying them flat on the table. 'What do you say, Julian?'

It was a straightforward bribe. If J.B. could buy off Julian and Robert, he would save his own life. It also offered Julian freedom from Bianca, because if he accepted she would leave him. She would never confine herself to that sort of income.

Julian didn't seem capable of speech. He clutched his glass with both hands, and then took one away to cover his wobbling chin.

'We must think about it, eh?' said J.B., granting him extra time.

'No need,' said Bianca. 'Julian and I think alike. He deserves better at your hands. Shabby treatment, indeed, for your only son. You talk of blood being thicker than water, but . . .'

'Julian?' asked his father.

'I . . .' Julian shook his head.

Robert reached for his inhaler. His eyes went from Julian to Bianca and back again. He cleared his throat. 'From my point of view, I wouldn't mind having the extra capital . . . but of course it's up to Julian to decide.'

Ruth Maudsley was crying, as was usual with her in times of stress.

Julian drained his glass and filled it again. His face was as pale as Charles. 'What about the yacht, father? And Whitestones? Then there's the flat in Paris, and . . .'

'You couldn't afford to keep them up. If I did leave them to you you would use them for a while, then they would become neglected and eventually have to be sold. I don't like to think of their being neglected. The Paris flat will be sold on my death, and the money will go to a French orphanage. Whitestones will be offered to the National Trust with a suitable endowment. The yacht will be sold and the money turned into the Trust Fund. Think about it; I am offering you a comfortable if not lavish income for life. I will even buy you into the Maudsley firm straight away, if you like. Provided I live long enough after that, there wouldn't be any death duties on the purchase price. I will guarantee you freedom from poverty, but I will not contribute to your unhappiness by offering you luxury.'

We all knew what he meant. I thought it was a very fair offer, and I had no doubt at all that it was a genuine one.

Julian looked as if he were about to be sick. His wife stood up abruptly, throwing her knife and fork on to the table. We all saw him stiffen under her eyes.

'If you make a Will like that,' he said to his father, 'then I'll contest it in the Courts. I am your only son and I deserve to be your only heir.'

There was a sigh of defeat from J.B. I suddenly felt cold. The faces of the conspirators bore identical expressions of grey implacability. Ruth had even stopped crying, now that everything was decided.

'Will you collect the plates, Susan?' asked Bianca. 'And bring in the syllabub and cheese.'

'Not for me,' said J.B.

'Just coffee then, Susan,' smiled Bianca, and led the way out of the dining-room. I wondered if Charles might help me to clear away, so that we could have a word together, but he stuck close to J.B.

By the time I had brought the coffee into the living-room everyone except Julian had settled down around the fire. Julian wandered around, not looking into anyone's face, fiddling with this and that. Charles looked remote; the profile of his head looked like a cameo, pale against the dark wood of the armoire. Robert alternatively inhaled and sneezed. Ruth was trying to hide her tear stains by putting too much powder on her face.

'Coffee?' I asked J.B., who appeared to be on the verge of dozing off. He looked right through me.

'Charles—did you cancel that meeting?'

'You know I did,' said Charles quietly.

'Can't trust anyone!' observed J.B. 'Do you think I don't know you pry through my papers?'

It was Bianca's chance, and she took it. 'Not only your papers, but your cheque-book, too. Have you had a look at your Bank Statement recently? Charles has been milking you for months.'

'What?' J.B. struggled to sit upright. 'What was that?'

'Didn't you know?' cooed Bianca. 'This precious Charles of yours, this son of your oldest friend, this so-clever personal assistant of yours has been putting blank cheques in with the household ones for you to sign. Then he makes them out payable to himself afterwards. Didn't you know he was doing it? He boasted to us that you didn't, but surely you must at least have suspected what was going on.'

'No!' said J.B., putting out a hand to stop her. His face contorted with pain as he bent over as if hinged at the hips, one hand clutching his suit jacket over his heart, and the other flailing the air.

I heard myself say, 'Heart pills—he must have some!' He groped in his pocket for a box while I ran for a glass of water. By the time I got back, he was able to sit up and take a pill. He didn't look as bad a colour as I had expected.

'Now listen,' Charles was saying.

'No, you listen to me, sir!' gasped J.B. 'If half what she says is true, then I'll see you join your father in jail. I'll put my accountants to work on this the moment I get back to Whitestones, and if there is as much as a single cheque unaccounted for . . . Get out of my sight!' He threw the glass of water at Charles. It missed, but some of the water splashed darkly against the leather of Charles' jacket.

'Out!' grinned Bianca, pointing to the front door.

Charles hesitated. 'His injection—you can see he's in a bad way, and not only from the heart attack . . .'

141

'I'll inject myself, thank you,' said J.B., struggling out of his chair. 'Julian, if you'll help me into your den for a moment . . .'

His face shining with strain, Julian took his father's arm and helped him, out of the living-room and into the den. Nobody moved until Julian returned, closing the door of the den behind him.

'How long?' asked Bianca.

'He's doing it now.'

Ruth shrieked. Robert slapped her. I could feel tears run down my own cheeks, as I turned on Charles.

'Do something—stop him, somehow! I didn't think you'd let him go through with it, even if he does prosecute over the cheques . . .'

'How can I stop him?' Charles asked, but he didn't look at me. He was concentrating on Julian.

We stood there, listening. There was no sound from the den.

'I can't bear it,' I said. 'We must get a doctor for him.' I started for the phone, only to have Robert thrust himself in front of me.

'You can't . . .'

'Stop her!'

Ruth screamed again. I panicked, side-stepped Robert and ran for the phone. Ruth, still screaming, tripped me and as I fell, she fell on top of me. Then Bianca was hissing something at Julian, who was arguing with

142

Charles. I could hear Robert wheezing above me, as I fought with Ruth.

'We can't let him die . . .'

'. . . get hold of her by that arm . . .'

'He's your father! For God's sake, Julian!'

'Bitch!'

Then something hit me on the head and the room went into a spiral around me. When it straightened out, I was sitting in the place recently occupied by J.B., and Ruth was cutting the telephone cord. The door of the den was now open. Julian came out, closely followed by Charles.

'Charles!' He looked across at me, concerned, but didn't rush to my side. He was one step behind Julian, crossing the hall to the door, urging him to do, or not do something. I heard the words . . . 'Doctor said . . .' and ' Maybe hours . . .' Julian was pressing the back of his hand to his upper lip. He looked tortured.

'Shut up, you!' said Robert, glowering over me.

'No!' cried Charles, catching Julian by the shoulder and forcing him to stand still. 'I won't stand for murder. I didn't really think you'd go through with it. I know you can't. Look— I'll take the blame for the cheques if you like, but . . . all you've got to do is phone for a doctor, get J.B. round, say there was some mistake . . . he'll never guess that you meant him any harm and then in due course you'll inherit . . .'

'I agree with Bianca that it's too late,' said Robert. 'J.B.'s too sharp a bird not to guess that that last injection was out of the ordinary. And even if we do switch bottles . . .'

'We've no choice,' said Ruth, her voice jerking. 'If we get a doctor and J.B. comes round, he'll prosecute Charles and Charles will be able to prove that he didn't put the money through his own account. No one will be able to prove that he did. But if the bank is asked to hand over those cheques to J.B., he'll see at once that they were made payable to us. The only way we can cover up the fraud is to allow J.B. to die.'

'Oh, Charles is in it up to his neck,' said Bianca. She was the only one in the room who didn't appear to be feeling the strain. 'The only way we could have got those cheques is through Charles, and even if he didn't benefit from them directly, he still committed a crime by obtaining them for us, and so he'll go to prison.'

'Prison or no,' said Charles, 'I'll not let him die. Now do you go for the doctor, Julian or do I?'

The two men stood toe to toe, glaring at each other. I willed Julian to give in. He did waver.

'You always had a special feeling for him, didn't you?' Charles didn't reply. 'Well . . . I suppose . . . but the phone—you can see we

144

can't phone.'

'We can take my car, and phone from down the road.'

Bianca slid her arm through her husband's, pressing herself against him as she whispered in his ear. Julian's face stilled. His back stiffened, and I knew we'd lost.

'Go if you like,' he said indifferently. 'I suppose it may help your case with the police if you call the doctor yourself. If you do succeed in reviving my father, and he raises the matter of who received the money from the cheques, then we shall say that you gave it to us so that we could repay the people who had suffered from your father's fraud.'

It sounded thin. I didn't like it, and I could see that Charles didn't either. There was something about the cocky set of Julian's head which hinted at knowledge undisclosed.

'All right,' said Charles. He looked and sounded defeated. He came over to me, and I stumbled to my feet.

'I'll come with you,' I said, and then had to steady myself so as not to fall. I'd been hit on the head once too often.

'Let her stay,' said Ruth unexpectedly. 'She's not fit to go tearing around.'

'Why—so she shall,' said Bianca. She put an arm round my shoulders, pulling me off balance and away from Charles. There was something about her ready agreement which puzzled me, but my head was aching too badly for me to be able to work it out.

'Well . . .' said Charles, looking unsure of himself for once. 'I'll only be five minutes, Sue, and it's true you don't look too good.' He glanced at his watch. 'Say ten minutes at the outside.'

We didn't even kiss or touch hands. He let himself out. We heard his car start up. I didn't even go to the window to wave goodbye.

'Let him get to the road,' said Ruth.

'Yes,' agreed Bianca. 'She was busy with something in the armoire. 'We don't want him blocking our drive.' She brought a complicated bit of electrical wiring out of the cupboard and set it on the coffee table. 'Sue—come and look at this, will you?'

I felt evil in the air, but couldn't work out where it came from.

She smiled up at me. I think it was the very first time I'd seen her look really pleased about something. 'Do you remember that we installed a radio set in Charles' car after he had his little spell in hospital? Well, that was no ordinary radio. It contained sufficient explosive to blow the car to fragments, and Charles with it. It has a radio-controlled detonator, and this . . .' She gestured to the box of tricks before her. 'Is it!' She grabbed my hand and selected a finger. 'Here—press the switch and send your lover to Kingdom Come!'

'No!' I screamed. 'Charles!'

146

'No good calling for him,' laughed Bianca, pulling on my finger. I clawed at her with my free hand, and Julian hastened to help his wife. He wound his long arms round me, forcing me towards the wicked instrument. I kicked and heard him yelp. I screamed. Ruth flung herself on my other arm; she was crying again. Robert danced around us, yelling ineffectively.

'Now!' screamed Ruth.

'Now!' smiled Bianca, and with one last effort she placed my finger into position and bore down on my hand with all her weight. The impact bruising my finger and grazed the skin. Julian and Bianca held me there, holding the key down—my hand pressing down the key to blow Charles to pieces until we heard a muffled explosion. Then Julian pulled himself off me, and Bianca released my hand. She looked exultant.

'It had to be,' said Robert. 'He would have betrayed us, otherwise.'

'We can blame him for everything now,' nodded Bianca. 'No need to switch the bottles back . . . if there is any doubt raised about the old man's death, we can say that he'd found out that Charles was fiddling the books, and had threatened to expose him. That would have given Charles sufficient motive to kill J.B. It ought to finish Oliver Ashton off, too, to hear that one of his sons is a murderer! And Mary Ashton! When I see her face . . .!' I

147

thought she was going to have hysterics, but she managed to control herself.

I was looking at Robert; he shrunk away from me. 'You must see we had to safeguard ourselves,' he explained.

'That's right,' said Ruth, mopping herself up. 'We couldn't trust Charles because he couldn't be bought with money, or subdued by violence. We could control him more or less while he thought you were in danger, but once the old man was dead and we had to release you, we couldn't be sure what he'd do.'

I took deep breaths, one after the other. Soon I would begin to feel, and to suffer. Now I could only think how unfair it had been that Charles should have had to die. I didn't recognise my voice when I started to speak.

'You killed him because he was loyal and couldn't be bought; because he was true to those he loved. You killed him out of envy, because he was everything that you are not. He brought you face to face with the dark corners of your souls, and you couldn't bear it. He showed you that an easy conscience is of more lasting value than all the money you've stolen. You fought him with all the weapons you had, and although he was hurt he wasn't beaten because he could still laugh and make love and be loved in his turn.' I had their full attention. 'Can any of you say that you truly love anyone else, or that you can laugh at a good joke, or even that you are loved? At

148

night, when you go to bed, do you sleep peacefully or do you dream of the harm you've done? Do you dream of a harmless, kindly old man locked away in a cold cell, cut off from his family, just because he tried to help Julian, here? Will you, Robert, ever be free from asthma? Your trouble is psychosomatic, isn't it? It's brought on by worry, and worry will never leave you now, not till the end of your days. And you, Ruth . . . can you look at the man you've married and not envy other women their loving husbands and children? Does Robert love you? No, of course not. He hates you because every time he looks at you he's reminded of what he's done. And you hate him because he cares nothing for you. And what about you, Julian? Can you face the long hours of the night alone in your bed without wondering if with another woman you might have been able to enjoy a normal relationship, if you might even have been loved for your own sake and not for your prospects of inheriting a fortune? Will you ever be able to sleep, without thinking of the harm you did your benefactor, Oliver Ashton, and how you've killed the only man who understood your faults and was able to love you in spite of them? How does it feel to have killed your father? And Bianca . . .'

'Yes?' she said, slit-eyed.

'I think I understand you now. You married Julian thinking he would be your passport to

149

an easy life. Perhaps you even loved him for himself once, but that was all over a long time ago. Perhaps you stopped loving him when the money started to run out, perhaps when you met the Ashtons and saw what it might mean to be loved by the genuine article. You fell in love with Charles. He was the same age as the man you'd married and he had many of the same physical characteristics, but Charles was a true Golden Boy, and once you'd seen him you knew Julian for what he was—a smudged carbon copy. Only Charles wasn't interested in you and let you see it . . .' How well I remembered Charles telling me that women of Rita's type bored him, and how closely Bianca approximated to that type! 'You never understood what Charles wanted in a woman. He never did try to make you; that was a lie you made up to save your face after he rejected you. So what you couldn't have, you set out to destroy, by involving him in the frame of the fraud case, by traducing him to J.B., by blackmail, and by torture. And the only result of your efforts was to throw me in Charles' way. Did you know that he shared my bed from the night he left hospital? Perhaps you guessed he was lost to you for good when you visited me in my flat? Perhaps that was when you decided that Charles had to die. He died because you couldn't bear to see him loved and be loved by anyone but yourself.'

The smile set rigid on her face, faded, and

returned. Whatever I said, she would not allow her mouth to reflect the bitterness I saw in her eyes. I opened the front door. The sun had come out, but there was a cold wind blowing.

'Where are you going?' Ruth pulled on my arm.

'To Charles of course. He always felt the cold so much. I must go to him, and cover him over with something warm. I'll sit with him until the police come.'

'Don't be stupid!' said Ruth. 'Why do you think we stopped you from going with him in the first place? There's no need for you to get involved. He's dead and discredited. Let's leave it at that; no one else need get hurt.' She pushed between me and the doorway, speaking to the others over my shoulder. 'She's shocked. Get her a cup of tea, or a drink; something to make her see sense.'

'Let me go to him,' I said, pleading with her. She was so much stronger than she looked, and I was hardly able to keep on my feet. 'It can't matter now what I do.'

'You don't understand,' said Ruth. 'You can't allow yourself to be associated with him any more, for your own sake. He's dead, and there's nothing you can do to help him now. You've got to think of yourself. Life must go on. You must pack up and get out of here before we call the doctor for J.B. Don't think about Charles; someone will find him, passing along the road, and inform the police in due course. You must go back to your own flat and forget what's happened. Behave yourself, and everything will be all right, but we don't want you weeping and wailing over Charles' body in your present state. Why, if the police were to get at you now . . .'

'She'll betray us, too!' hissed Robert. 'You should have let her go with Charles.'

'She'll be all right, if she only pulls herself together.'

'You can see she won't. She doesn't care about anything . . .'

'That's right,' I said. 'I don't care about anything any more. I just want to be with Charles, that's all.'

A long, thin arm caught me round the waist and hauled me away from the door. Julian, breathing hard.

'There's a car coming up the drive—can't you hear it?'

Robert was peering through the window, his face reflecting shocked disbelief. 'The man from the Fraud Squad? What . . . I don't understand!'

In a flurry of movement, I was pushed and pulled to the centre of the room.

'The Old Man—he's dead?'

'. . . must be. Leave him where he is . . . we can say we tried to phone . . .'

'Put her in the freezer!' That was Bianca's voice lifting clear of the others. 'I checked there's plenty of room for her. We can put something heavy on top so that she can't get out. We can deal with her later, when the police have gone. No one will hear her if she screams, it's so well insulated . . .'

'She might die!'

'So? We stage a little accident in her flat later on . . .'

'No!' I tried to scream and had a cushion held over my face. I fought, but hands grabbed me from every angle, and I was bundled through the kitchen and into the utility room as the doorbell rang.

'Up-sa-daisy!' said Bianca. I was swung up and then down, hitting the frozen packets of food with such a thump that all the breath was knocked out of me. As I tried to struggle to my knees, the heavy lid of the freezer thudded down. I tried to heave it up, hunching myself against it, but it would not move. The chilly atmosphere bit at my hands, face and legs. The packets of frozen food were frosted with ice, which grated and stuck to my skin. I screamed and heard the sound return to me, shockingly muted.

'Charles!'

Tears came then. I shook and shivered. The cold began to grip through my clothes. I roused myself to attack the lid again, but it was no good. I collapsed wearily. I couldn't fight any more. I didn't particularly want to, now that Charles was dead. Soon I would be dead too, and that would be the end of that.

SIX

I was only half conscious when the lid was wrenched upwards and someone hauled me out of the freezer with the minimum of ceremony. Hard, cruelly hard hands brushed down my arms and legs and forced me to stand; I clutched at soft, supple leather and moaned, was picked up and hurtled through the air . . .

I gagged on the spirit poured down my throat.

'More!' said a voice I seemed to have known, a long time ago. The rim of a flask grated against my teeth. Whoever was holding the flask was quite determined that I should get more whisky down me. I drank, and felt fire burn my gullet, and chase down into my ribs, competing with the chill that was convulsing my body in rhythmic shivers. My hands and legs flamed as someone chafed them. My cheek burned. Someone pulled my hair up and wrapped me round in a cocoon of soft leather that smelt new. My nose was pressed into soft, warm wool.

Cautiously I opened my eyes. I wasn't wearing my glasses, but I knew that sweater. It was one of Charles' favourites. I was sitting on Charles' knee in the kitchen, and J.B. was peering into my face from a distance of six inches as he chafed my hands. He looked perfectly fit and very anxious.

'It's all right!' said Charles, in a voice which informed me that everything was very far from all right with him. I discovered that he was trembling, too. I pulled my hands away from J.B. and started to feel Charles all over.

'You're dead!' I said absurdly. 'You must be damaged, at least. Perhaps . . . are your legs all right?' I had a vision of Charles with his legs blown off, lying in a wrecked car. The memory of the unfortunate victim of the industrial accident, who had been in the same ward at the hospital as Charles, floated through my mind.

'Of course not!' he said angrily. 'Don't be stupid, Sue! You didn't expect me to take a gift of a radio from them without wondering what was behind it? I had it to pieces the first day I took possession of the car, discovered the explosive device, and wrote to David for instructions as to how to deal with it. Then I bought an identical radio set to install in my car, and put the original, lethal set in that old toolshed at the bottom of the garden here. It made a fine noise when it went up, didn't it?' He captured both my hands and held them so tightly that I almost screamed with pain. In fact, he was holding me so tightly I couldn't have moved if I'd wanted to do so. I was only thankful it wasn't necessary. I began to weep into his sweater.

J.B. chirruped something about giving me more whisky, and Charles told him not to be more of a fool than he could help. I had not been mistaken about one thing, anyway; Charles was in a right royal rage about something. I soon found out what.

Someone thrust my spectacles at me. It was Ronald, looking as calm as if he were about to attend a board-room meeting, complete with brief-case.

'Ronald!' said Charles, threateningly, 'I thought I told you to see that nothing happened to Sue while I took the car out of sight. She might have been killed.'

'Sorry about that,' Ronald apologised to me. 'I was helping Uncle John out of the study window, and by the time I'd done that, you were in the freezer.'

'Don't fuss!' said J.B., patting Charles on the shoulder. 'You can see she's going to be all right.'

'No thanks to you two!' growled Charles.

'You should have heard what she had to say about you, when she thought you were dead,' volunteered J.B., trying to soften Charles' mood.

'Thank you,' snapped Charles. 'I'll hear it later from Sue, if she wishes to repeat it.'

Ronald offered me a handkerchief. 'Would

you like to borrow this? Jane never has a handkerchief on her in moments of crisis.'

I took the handkerchief and blew my nose, understanding that only by showing signs of returning to normal would Charles be able to calm down.

J.B. gave me another anxious smile, rather as one offers a strange dog a hand to sniff at. 'You were quite taken in by our little quarrel, then? You didn't guess we had it all worked out beforehand?'

'It did cross my mind that you recovered from that heart attack rather quickly,' I said, trying to smile back. 'Am I to understand that you knew what was going to happen all along? And about the cheques?'

'Of course. Charles couldn't have slipped that trick across me even if he'd tried, and naturally he was sensible enough not to try. As for the injection which I gave myself after lunch, that was insulin, as usual. The bottle which Julian gave Charles has been sent to an analyst.'

'I'm sorry about Julian,' said Charles. 'I thought he'd crack, right up to the last.'

'He was inadequate from birth; as Sue said—a smudged carbon copy of the real thing. He was given every chance to back out, both by me and by you. Now he must take his punishment with the others.'

'Punishment?' I sat upright, but didn't try to get off Charles' knees. 'The Fraud Squad were coming. That's why they had . . .'

All three men were smiling at me, as one smiled indulgently at a small child for committing a solecism.

'Didn't you guess?' asked Charles. 'It's really so very simple . . .'

'. . . to one of your devious turn of mind!' barked J.B.

'Well, it was dicy in parts,' admitted Ronald. 'But I don't think any of us can actually be charged with an offence, the way we've handled it.'

He approached the door to the living-room, and set it ajar so that we could overhear the conversation there. A strange man was talking.

'. . . at your office yesterday morning, and what we found there seems to confirm the claim made . . .'

'Of course, Inspector,' Robert was talking. 'I gathered you had some query to raise with me, but I was busy with a client, and unfortunately Mr. Brenner was unable to be at the office yesterday. Naturally, anything we can do to help . . . I'll be happy to meet you at the office tomorrow morning, so that we can clear this matter . . . as you can see, we are just having a coffee after lunch, and . . .'

'I must apologise for breaking in on you on a Sunday, but the nature of our information . . .'

'You wanted to see me?' That was Julian's

158

voice. 'Otherwise why come here, to my home?'

'If there is somewhere we could go for a quiet chat? If the ladies will excuse us?'

'Not on my account,' stated Bianca. 'Please sit down, Inspector.'

'I used to work for my husband.' That was Ruth. 'I was Miss James, before. Perhaps you remember me, from the Ashton fraud case? I would prefer to stay, too.'

'Well, now. A couple of days ago we received a formal complaint from a client of yours that over a period of several months he has been sending you cheques for various sums, on the understanding that you were to invest it for him. On checking through his records, he finds that although the cheques have been cashed, he doesn't appear to have received any share certificates. At first he thought you might just have been holding them for him. He wrote to you a week ago, asking whether this was the case; remembering the Ashton fraud, he added that he must have a satisfactory explanation from you within four days, or he would go to the police. He has not heard from you, and accordingly asked us to investigate.'

'What nonsense!' That was Robert's voice. 'He's a nut, obviously. Our books are perfectly in order. You know that they are, because you checked them at the time of old man Ashton's frauds.'

'You don't understand. The cheques concerned were sent to you within the last five months since Oliver Ashton was convicted of fraud.'

'That's just not possible!'

'I'm afraid it is. His letters are all on file at your office, to prove it.'

'Inspector!' This was Bianca. 'What is the name of this client?'

'Mr. John Brenner, of Whitestones.'

There was a tense silence next door. I peeped at J.B. and Ronald. J.B. was smiling, and Ronald's finger was poised over the dish of syllabub which I had left on the kitchen table. As I watched, he dipped his finger in, licked it, and registered pleased surprise. His eye started to wander round the kitchen, looking for a spoon. Charles was concentrating on the conversation next door; he was very tense.

'John Brenner . . . my father?' Julian sounded hoarse. 'But he's never been a client of Robert's. He's always made his own investments through a London . . . The idea of his putting business through us is absurd.'

'Your records show that he sent you a total of . . .' Charles' lips moved in concert, detailing the amount, '. . . twenty thousand, two hundred and thirty-seven pounds, for which Mr. Brenner has received neither acknowledgement nor Share Certificates.'

'There's no proof . . .'

160

'I have been shown copies of Mr. John Brenner's bank statements for the last six months, which prove that the cheques have been cashed on his account. I have also seen the covering letters he wrote you, which are in a file under his name in your office.'

'It just can't be!' wailed Ruth. 'There's no such file for him!'

'I've seen it!' said the Inspector tonelessly. 'Yesterday morning.'

'Charles!' This was Bianca. 'This is Charles' doing! I can feel it! Inspector, you know that Oliver Ashton had . . . has a son, a very bright rogue. He was forced to resign his job in London after the fraud case, and went to John Brenner for a job. This is Charles' way of getting back at Robert and Julian for taking over his father's firm—oh, quite legitimately! I mean, Robert bought the firm quite legitimately from Oliver Ashton, when . . . I see it all! Charles has put the cheques in front of J.B. when he's signing a lot and won't notice . . . then he's made them out himself afterwards. Of course they've passed through J.B.'s account! You'll find the money in Charles' bank account, unless he's managed to get it out of the country already.'

'I'm afraid that won't do. You see, Mr. Brenner is one of the few people I know who insist on the bank's returning all cancelled cheques to him. He started doing this some while back. He has isolated the relevant

161

cheques, and handed them over to me. They are made out either to Mr. Robert Maudsley, or to Mr. Julian Brenner. I have also received photographic copies of Mr. and Mrs. Julian Brenner's joint bank account statements for the last two years.'

'How on earth? Charles couldn't have . . .'

'I don't know how, Mrs. Brenner. They were dropped through my letter-box at home in the early hours of the morning. There don't appear to be any fingerprints on them. They were in a plain business-type envelope, of the type you can buy anywhere, and there was no address or superscription of any kind on the envelope. My wife opened it, in fact, thinking it was a bill from the newsagent's.'

'Well, what if you do have a copy of our bank statements?' asked Julian. 'I still don't see why you come here . . .'

'At regular intervals over the last five months you seem to have paid in either the full amount of one of the cheques sent to you by Mr. John Brenner, and then reimbursed some party or parties unknown with half the amount, or have paid in exactly one half of the amount yourself. It looks as though the money sent you by Mr. John Brenner was shared out between you and someone else, don't you think? I assume that the other person is Mr. Maudsley here, which is why, when I couldn't find Mr. Maudsley at home this morning, I came on here. Now do either of you have any comment to make?'

So that's why David had taken such a risk! He'd come over from Ireland specially to photograph the bank statements so as to link Julian with receipt of the cheques; then he'd handed the negatives in at Whitestones. Charles had developed and printed them up over-night, and delivered them to the Inspector's home at precisely the right moment. No wonder he hadn't slept last night.

Ronald set down his spoon with a sigh of satisfaction, having reduced the level of the syllabub in the bowl considerably. J.B. was brushing pastry flakes from his finger tips; he'd been at a tin of jam tarts I'd made yesterday.

'That money,' said Bianca, 'was a gift from John Brenner to Julian and Robert. It can't have anything to do with—nothing to do with the purchase of shares. The money we paid into our bank account was to purchase a partnership in the Maudsley firm for my husband. You see, my father-in-law has been very pleased with the way Julian has been settling down at the firm, and he thought it would be a nice gesture to buy him a partnership. Charles brought us the cheques personally, because . . .'

'I saw Mr. Charles Ashton yesterday and he told me he and his boss were to lunch here today with you. Perhaps we might ask them to join us just to confirm what you say.'

Robert began to wheeze; I could hear him from the kitchen. Charles sighed softly, and bent his head to rest against mine. J.B. reached out to pick a strand of turkey from the carcase.

'Charles left early,' said Julian. 'He quarrelled with my father and left. He said there was something the matter with his car, and that he wanted to take it to a garage on his way home. As a matter of fact, we heard a loud bang just after he left, and wondered if he'd come to grief. We were just discussing whether we ought to go and have a look when you arrived.'

'That's right,' said Ruth. 'Almost like an explosion.'

'Something leaking from the engine? He said he smelt something.'

'I saw nothing like that on the way,' said the Inspector stolidly. 'No crashed cars, or explosions, or any other such nonsense. So Mr. Ashton was here, but isn't now and can't confirm your story. He had a quarrel with Mr. John Brenner, you say? What about? Well, I don't suppose it's relevant. What we have to do now is ask Mr. John Brenner whether he meant those cheques as a personal gift or not. Where is he?'

'He wasn't feeling too good after lunch,' said Bianca. 'He had this quarrel, and somehow . . . he went to lie down in Julian's den. Shall I go and ask him if he's feeling well enough to join us?'

'I'll go,' said the Inspector. 'This door?' There was a pause, and then the Inspector's voice came back, angry. 'There isn't anyone here. Is this supposed to be a joke?'

'He must be!' screamed Ruth, as usual losing her cool.

'Let me see . . .'

'Where could he have gone? He was lying down when I last saw him.' That was Julian. 'He couldn't have moved, I tell you! He was in a coma . . .'

'A coma?' repeated the Inspector. 'That's not what you said before. Sergeant, I think we'd better call for reinforcements.'

A new voice overrode agitated protests. 'The phone cord's been cut clean through, sir!'

'So I see. Now precisely what is going on here, may I ask? There's money turning up here, there and everywhere, and two people missing . . . no, wait a minute! There's seven cups of coffee poured out; four on the tray here—that's for you lot—and three more I can see hiding in that big cupboard over there. You four, Mr. John Brenner and Mr. Charles Ashton make six. Whose was the seventh cup?'

'Someone who came to cook lunch for us,' said Bianca. 'She left after lunch.'

'Do you normally invite a cook to sit down and have coffee with you after a meal? I'd like

165

to meet this paragon. Where does she live?'

'She . . .'

'. . . she might be home by now, or she might . . .'

'She was going off somewhere for the afternoon, I think. To see her parents. I don't know where they live.'

'I think,' said the Inspector, 'that it's more than time that we adjourned to the Station. Sergeant, phone from the car outside, will you, and . . .'

'Our cue,' said Charles, sliding me off his knee and recovering his jacket. Ronald and J.B. filed through into the sitting-room behind us. Ruth saw us first. She rammed her fingers into her mouth and shrieked. Robert went a peculiar shade of purplish-red, and reached for his inhaler. Bianca whirled round, her eyes dilated. I saw that she at least now understood everything.

'May I ask . . .?' This was the Inspector, a heavy-faced, dark man, squat and powerful. 'Mr. John Brenner, Mr. Charles Ashton and Mr. Ronald Ashton. Interesting. And the young lady?'

'Allow me to explain!' said J.B. He took the Inspector by the arm, and led him into Julian's den. The Sergeant had disappeared, presumably to phone in for reinforcements.

'We've been conned!' said Bianca, in a surprised voice. Julian sank into a chair and covered his face with his hands. I think,

166

although I can't be quite sure, that he was crying.

Ronald advanced to inspect the electrical device on the table. He opened his brief-case, eased on a pair of gloves, produced a large plastic bag, wrapped it round the lethal box of tricks and put it into his bag. After that he removed his gloves, sat down, and began to sort some documents on to the table.

'Shall we recap for you?' asked Charles. 'Three attempted murders, one kidnapping, one case of torture and one of assault . . .'

'We'll all get life!' gasped Ruth, crying as usual.

Bianca raised one hand wearily, and smiled. It wasn't a nice smile, it showed her gums. 'I don't think that's the point, is it Charles? What you really want is to get your father out of jail. Am I right? That's why you gave us the cheques, to frame us into a situation similar to the one for which we got your father. And I suppose it was Ronald, with his knowledge of office routine, who did a little breaking and entering to plant that incriminating file of letters from J.B. in the right filing cabinet at the right time.

'Not breaking and entering,' said Ronald apologetically. 'Nobody asked me for my keys when I was thrown out of the firm. Merely trespass.'

'So who got the photographs of our bank statements . . . Sue? No, it couldn't have been

Sue. She hasn't got a camera, and . . .'

'David. He was the telephone engineer who called to rectify a fault on your line yesterday morning; a fault created by Sue, acting on my instructions. But you won't be able to prove it, I'm afraid.'

'No, I'm quite sure we won't,' agreed Bianca. 'So—how much?'

'You sign these,' said Charles, as Ronald adjusted his glasses and handed out some typed documents. 'They're identical—just read them through and sign at the bottom. Ronald and Sue can witness them.'

'Just what are we supposed to be confessing to?' asked Bianca, taking her copy with a steady hand.

'The original fraud, that's all.'

'No mention of attempted murder, or grievous bodily harm or anything like that?'

'Certainly not. Neither J.B. nor I believe that the present system of locking people away for decades is a good one. You'll be punished in other ways; by loss of status, income and reputation. I don't know what you'll get for fixing the fraud case on my father, but I don't suppose it will be more than the seven years he was given, and it may be less. Of course, you'll have to refund the money you stole as well . . .'

'You know we can't do that! It's nearly all . . .'

'That's where this second document comes

in,' said Charles. He took a legal-looking wodge of paper from Ronald and handed it to Robert. 'Now the twenty thousand which I gave you by way of J. B . . .'

'By way of . . .? You mean that the money was yours all the time? Where did you get it from?'

'You set me next to J.B. to break me; all you succeeded in doing was giving me the chance of a lifetime to make money on the 'Change by keeping my ears and eyes open and apeing his methods. As I earned it, I gave it to him and he gave me a cheque in return . . . which I paid over to you. Don't worry about that last cheque for three thousand, by the way. You may not have been able to pay it in yet, but I assure you it will be honoured. Now I suggest we regularise the position in the manner suggested by J.B. Robert sells the firm back to me, for the amount he paid for it. For twenty thousand pounds, which he has already received. Robert?'

The sound of Robert's wheezes filled the room. Then he lunged forward, took the contract and signed it. His hand shook. Ronald and I witnessed his signature while Charles stood over us like an avenging angel.

Just as we finished, the Sergeant, a boyish, red-faced lad, came back into the house, gave us a puzzled look and asked for the Inspector.

'In that room,' said Charles, pointing.

'These good people here are just on the point of signing statements for you, and will be ready to accompany you to the Station in a moment.' The Sergeant went into the den and closed the door behind him.

'Because if you don't sign,' said Charles, speaking in a thread of a voice, 'then we might start remembering all sorts of things which might prove difficult for you to explain away. Like the matter of a forged Will, and a bottle of digitalin with Julian's fingerprints on it . . .'

'My God!' screamed Ruth. 'He wore gloves when he took them! He never touched them with his bare hands himself, and that means . . .'

'Precisely! Your fingerprints, my dear Ruth, are delightfully clear on the Will, but I believe the others' are also well represented. Then there is that little piece of apparatus which Ronald has just confiscated, and the matter of where I was and what happened to me before I landed in hospital. Our memories will be conveniently faulty on the subject of all these things, if you clear my father and accept what's coming to you.'

'You still can't link us to the fraud case unless we sign,' said Bianca.

'I'm afraid we can,' smiled Charles. 'Didn't you hear the Inspector say he got copies of your bank statements for the last couple of years? The payment you received—nineteen thousand pounds—from Robert Maudsley for helping with the fraud case and subsequent frame shows up beautifully. You banked the sum six months and three weeks ago. I expect the Inspector will want to see Robert's bank statements now, won't he? Sign or not, you're finished. But I'd prefer you to sign because I want my father home quickly. Remember I've got to come down to the Station with you now, to corroborate the fact that J.B. was acting middleman for me in buying the firm; if you don't sign, then I might find myself digressing on to all sorts of other topics when I make my statement.'

'We'll sign,' said Bianca. She took the pen from Robert, skimmed through the statement, made a face, and signed. The others signed too. I had been right in thinking that Julian had been crying.

A second police car shot up the drive as the Inspector, J.B., and the Sergeant came out of Julian's den. All three were looking thoughtful.

Charles handed the statements to the Inspector, who glanced down them without comment. No doubt J.B. had been putting him in the picture.

'I'll get my coat,' said Ruth. Robert watched her put it on and then, clumsily put his arm round her shoulders and gave them a squeeze. It was the first gesture I'd ever seen him make towards her, but she was too enclosed in her misery to respond. She shook off his arm and walked out of the house without looking back. Suddenly Robert looked too small for his clothes. He flicked a quick glance at us to see if we'd notice the incident, and followed her.

'I must lock up,' announced Bianca.

'We will see to that,' said the Inspector. 'You will give us your permission to have a look around, won't you?'

'To search my house?'

Julian laughed unhappily. 'No longer our house, dear. It will have to be sold to repay what we stole.'

'Not my house,' she repeated, beginning to realise that her life as a rich and elegant woman was over. She revolved, looking round the room, impressing it on her memory, bidding it farewell. Whatever happened, Bianca wasn't going to return to the scene of her defeat. She stopped at J.B. 'You do realise that you are not only sending your precious son to jail, but also breaking up his marriage?'

'For the first, I am sorry. For the second, you cannot expect me to grieve.'

'And your money? I suppose you'll leave it to Charles?'

'Already done,' said J.B. Charles started and would have spoken, but J.B. silenced him with a raised hand. 'Charles knew nothing of it, and I suppose I shall have difficulty getting him to accept it. No, let me finish, Charles. I've made you my heir because I like the thought of my money going to someone who will know how to look after it.'

'So Charles gets everything,' mused Bianca. 'The money, the house, the yacht, the girl . . . I knew he was the sort to go far, as soon as I saw him. I hope . . . I wish . . . you shouldn't have refused me, Charles!'

Before Julian could stop her, she reached up, wound her arms round behind Charles' neck, and pressed her mouth to his. We all stood there and watched, too shocked to do anything about it. Charles hardly seemed to notice what she was doing at first, and then he put his hands up to break her grip, and pushed her away from him. Her lipstick left a garish stain on his mouth, so that he looked as if he'd bitten his lip.

She took one step back, and then another. I couldn't bear to look at her face. Julian caught at her arm. He spoke her name. I heard her laugh . . . and then she was gone, and he, poor fool, ran after her.

'It is not wise,' said Charles conversationally, 'to frame a man for a crime if he has three able-bodied sons to defend him.'

Ronald snapped shut the lock on his briefcase, and Charles shuddered as if waking from a bad dream.

*   *   *

Of course, it wasn't the end of the matter. J.B.

arranged for Julian to be represented by a solicitor, and even found him a job of sorts until the trial came up. He visits Julian every other month in prison, but won't talk about it. Bianca went to a hotel until the trial, and sent the bills to J.B. That marriage is definitely over.

As far as we were concerned, our involvement with the police ended when Charles and J.B. left the Station that afternoon, but Charles still had one more battle to fight.

I had been waiting for him in his car, knitting and listening to the radio. I felt half asleep, but forgot my own troubles when Charles came. His face was incandescent with fatigue. He got into the car and sat there, playing with his keys.

'I've failed, you know,' he said. 'I've cleared Dad. I've got the family firm back, and I've made a lot of money, but it's too late. He'll be dead before the summer's out.'

'Now that's nonsense . . .'

'He gave up when he was forced to plead guilty. I could see it in his face when he told us what he'd agreed to do. He'd been fighting the cancer before that; he'd wanted to live, to see David's three little girls again, to see Jane's baby, to see me settled. But after that night he stopped fighting. Mother thinks he had just resigned himself to the situation, and that's why he was so passive. She said it was because he'd got used to prison routine, and being known by his surname and number. I tried to fool myself that was what it was, too . . . but I'm not much good at fooling myself. I ought to have thought of something which would have worked more quickly . . . No, the damage was done that first night! I must remember that.' He sighed, and fitted the key in the ignition. 'Another thing Jane's baby is no good. It moved late and feebly. She's had trouble all along. She may carry it to term, but if it isn't still-born, it won't live long. She knows it; I see her put one hand on her stomach to try to feel movement, and all the time her eyes are frightened . . . She thinks she's let Ronald down. She looks at him as if expecting him to stop loving her because she can't bear him a healthy child.'

'You have an over-active imagination. You can't possibly know these things for certain. You've been over-working. You'll feel better . . .'

'And you hate J.B., don't you? You won't share me with him; I could read that in your face as soon as you met him. So I must leave him, and he will die, too.'

I didn't know what to say to that. If he'd understood that I hated J.B., then he'd also understood that J.B. hated me.

He tried to start the car, and flooded the engine. 'I must get a licence tomorrow,' he said. 'Will your parents be very angry if we get

175

married without any fuss, quickly? Strange to think I've never even met them. One thing— they won't like me. How could they? I've no job now, no home to offer you, and I can be difficult to live with. But at least we'll have sons.'

'How many?' I asked, trying to break his mood.

'How the hell should I know?' he asked irritably. He tried to start the engine again, failed, and handed me the keys. 'You'd better drive—I'm bushed.'

*   *   *

The Sue Stephens of this world don't usually get invitations to stay at places like Whitestones; they buy a ticket to go over it on Open Days. The drive was half a mile long. On one side of the house lay a heated outdoor swimming pool, tennis courts, a croquet lawn, a formal maze and a rose garden. Then there was a walled vegetable garden, a paddock, and stabling converted to flats for some of the staff, with garages beneath. The house itself was early nineteenth century, stuffed with antique furniture and portraits of heavy-faced English gentry. There was also a lot of valuable china scattered around the place in display cabinets. It smelt like a museum. I found it cold in spite of the central heating; but then, I wasn't predisposed to like it.

Charles handed me over to Mrs. Green, a black-clad housekeeper, who showed me to a luxurious guest-room where I might wash and brush up. Unasked, she found me a new pair of tights, since my own were in shreds owing to the rough treatment they'd received that day. Her manners were almost perfect, but I felt she was making an inventory of my clothing and would report to the other servants on everything she saw.

Drinks were dispensed in the vast Blue sitting-room, with J.B. jocularly presiding, and Mary Ashton alternately laughing and crying with joy. The phone rang, and it was David, wanting to hear all the details. Mary Ashton couldn't sit down, she was so happy.

'Susan—our little heroine!' she cried, when she saw me. She almost ran towards me, with arms outstretched. It was beautifully done and possibly even genuine. I tried not to resent being called 'Susan' or 'little'. She pressed her scented cheek to mine, and introduced me to Jane, whose wan face and big brown eyes were also showing both tears and smiles. I liked Jane on sight, because she was as plain as I. She had heavy eyebrows which needed thinning out, and she wore the very minimum of make-up. When she spoke, it was in such a shy voice that you had to bend over her to catch her words. I felt we were going to get on well together.

We processed through a gallery hung with

blue-green tapestries to the panelled dining-room, lit with great clusters of candles in massive silver-plated stands. This was the smaller of two dining-rooms, J.B. told me, and used for intimate, family affairs. The silverware was Georgian, the plates hand-painted and the glass Waterford. I thought the food elaborate and over-rich, and it occurred to me to wonder whether J.B. ought to be eating it, if he were on a diet . . . didn't diabetics have to diet? I decided it was none of my business, anyway.

Charles was treated as the son of the house already. He hardly touched his wine, and ate nothing. He couldn't share his mother's delight. He'd paid too high a price, personally, for his success, to be able to laugh with her. And she did laugh; she talked the whole of dinner, wittily, bubbling over; then catching up her handkerchief to dab at her eyes as tears spilled, and laughing at herself for crying. She chided Charles for being lumpish and stupid. I stiffened, and noticed that J.B. did, too. Charles and I were sitting one on either side of J.B., and now I saw that J.B. was watching Charles as closely as I.

'Make an effort, Charles!' cried Mary.

Charles did his best to rouse himself. He joined in the chatter for a moment or two, and then fell silent again. J.B. turned to look at me, in calculating fashion, and I stared back at him. We didn't exactly declare a truce, but in

178

that exchange of glances each admitted that we were worried about Charles, and would do our best to protect him until he had recovered his usual spirits. And it seemed, oddly enough, as if Charles did need protection. His mother seemed to think he was incapable of looking after himself. For instance . . .

'John dear,' she was saying to J.B., 'That foolish boy of mine—has he got terribly in debt with you over this business of buying back the firm? He said something about having earned the money, but of course I can't believe that . . . !'

'Charles is not a moron!' snapped J.B., and then softened into a smile for her. 'No, my dear. He's not in my debt. In fact, I believe I owe him three weeks' salary as of this minute.'

'I suppose you mean to cancel his debts because he saved your life, but of course we will repay you . . . '

'Nonsense! Charles will you explain, or shall I?' Charles shook his head. Now and then he looked across the table at me, as if he wanted to ask me something, but couldn't in front of the others.

'Well,' said J.B., firmly drawing attention back to himself, 'When Charles first approached me for a job he was in something of a dilemma, because the scheme he'd evolved demanded my active co-operation, and he didn't think he could get it without proof. If he'd told me straight out, for

179

instance, that he suspected my son Julian of being a crook and having framed Oliver for the fraud, I'd have thrown him out on his ear. Look at it from my point of view . . . one of my oldest friends, in whom I could have sworn I could have placed every confidence, had not only been arrested for fraud, but had confessed to it! Then the cleverest of his sons, whom I had last seen established in a good job in London, swanning around in a Mercedes, with a dozen suits in his wardrobe, comes to me for a job right out of the blue. Not only had he traded in his car for a cheap job, but also his wrist-watch, and he didn't appear to have much left in the way of clothes. Naturally I was suspicious. Even if Julian hadn't been hinting that Charles had been involved in the fraud case, I'd have been suspicious.

'He said he'd lost money on the 'Change. It was possible, of course, but somehow it didn't sound right. I offered him the job at half his previous salary and he took it on condition he could use any information he came across while working for me, to help him recoup his losses. That amused me! The nerve of the lad! So I took him on. I'll admit I gave him a rough time at first, because my confidence in him had been shaken. I didn't know what to believe. Then about a month after he started with me, he brought me a cheque for £1,500, payable to me, and explained that he wanted me to pay that into my bank account, and give

180

him an open cheque for the same amount. I asked why. He said he believed that Robert and Ruth had framed his father for the fraud case. He said that it was at Robert's suggestion that he, Charles, had applied to me for a job, and that Robert wanted him to milk me. He didn't mention Julian's name at all, which was wise of him. Even so, I said I didn't buy it. He said it would be easy to prove; if I paid the cheque for £1,500 into my bank account, and gave Charles a cheque for the same amount, we should see where it turned up by asking the bank to return all cancelled cheques to me in future. Charles filled it out for £1,500, but left the payee's name open. He made the point that if Robert paid the cheque into his own bank account and didn't ask me for an explanation as to why I should pay him so much money out of the blue, then there was my proof.

'I agreed. I had nothing to lose, and I'll admit I was curious. Charles' cheque was cleared through into my account, I gave Charles my cheque, and it was duly cleared through into Robert's account. I was all for calling in the police there and then, but Charles wouldn't have it. One more cheque, he said. This time it was for five thousand pounds . . .'

'But did he really earn that much?'

'Of course. He has a natural flair for handling money, forecasting trends . . . Well, what he didn't tell me was that that second cheque was to be made payable to Julian. He let me find it out for myself. The old man stared down at the table, placing his hands together and folding the fingers of one hand over the fingers of the other. Then he looked up, banishing memory of the shock which that cheque had given him. 'I didn't want to believe that my son was involved, but as soon as I saw that cheque, I guessed what had been going on. After that, Charles told me everything he knew about the fraud case, the blackmail, and the way they wanted him to obtain money from me. He told me his plan, and I agreed to co-operate. I wanted to lend him the rest of the money he needed, but he wouldn't have it; he had to buy the firm back himself.'

'But surely,' I asked, 'the law doesn't allow a criminal to profit from his crimes nowadays? Couldn't he have got Robert to return the firm by going to the Courts, once he'd proved fraud?'

'Not so easy,' said Ronald. 'Dad sold the firm to Robert in a perfectly straightforward manner, and it might have taken the legal profession years to get the rights and wrongs of the situation sorted out if we'd left it to them. This way Mother still has the twenty thousand invested in Collett Cosmetics, and I can still walk into Dad's old office tomorrow morning and start getting the business back to normal again.'

'But it's Charles who really owns the firm now?' asked Mary. 'How strange that seems! I wonder what Oliver will have to say to that; he never thought Charles would settle down and work in the firm . . .'

'God forbid!' put in the usually placid Ronald, and everyone laughed.

'It would never work, Mother,' said Charles. 'I couldn't work with Ronald. I'd drive him crazy. No, I'll sell it back to Ronald. We'll work out terms . . .'

'You'll sell it back to your father, you mean,' said Mary, laughing.

Charles looked at me, as if daring me to dispute her belief that Oliver Ashton was going to come out of prison the same man as before.

Jane relieved the tension. 'Then what will you do, Charles? Go back to London?'

'I might. Not to the same firm, of course. I left under something of a cloud; they don't like their bright young executives to walk out at a moment's notice . . . There was some talk once of my putting in for a job in Brussels . . . I don't know . . .'

J.B. opened his mouth to say something, then shut it again. I could almost feel his pain as he recognised that he'd lost Charles. He sat rock still to hide it from us, but I saw his distress, and so did Charles. The three of us sat in silence while the others laughed and joked together.

'Well,' said Mary. 'All's well that ends well. I'm sure, John, that you'll be only too glad to get rid of my troublesome son here. He can come back with us tonight to Green Gables . . .'

'He's welcome to stay here,' said J.B., not looking at Charles.

'Yes, I know,' said Charles. 'You know how I feel about that. I'm very, very sorry.'

'At least you'll accept a new car for saving my life several times over. Another Mercedes?' Charles shook his head. 'But you'll accept it if I make Sue a gift of it?'

'Ah, that!' Charles smiled across at me, and then at J.B. It was a shadow of a smile, but a very sweet one. 'Yes, if you give it to Sue, I'll accept it.'

Danger! whispered a voice in my ear. I'd underestimated J.B. By offering to give me a valuable car, he had told Charles that he was willing to share him with me. I could see that Charles wanted me to be equally magnanimous, but I couldn't do it. I stood up. It was rude, and abrupt and all of those things that one shouldn't do in other people's houses, but I wanted to get Charles away quickly before anything else happened.

'I'm awfully tired,' I said. 'Would everyone be offended if I just took Charles away? It's not far to my flat, and in the morning he can think what we ought to do next.'

Charles stood, too. I don't suppose anyone but J.B. and I noticed that he had to lean on the table to get himself upright. 'I'll get my shaving things,' he said. 'The rest can wait till tomorrow.'

'Why not show Sue your quarters, now that she's here?' said J.B., also getting to his feet. It seemed only natural for him to put one arm round Charles' shoulders as he walked with us to the door. The others were directed back to the Blue drawing-room for coffee while J.B. shepherded us to a lift which led out of the main hall and took us up to the first floor without our having to trouble with the stairs.

'This way,' said J.B., throwing open double doors to reveal an opulently furnished sitting-room. 'Office through there, bathroom and kitchen this way, bedroom beyond. He's got his own outside phone, of course, as well as an extension from the house phone. I had thought of turning all this side of the house into one self-contained unit; the rooms under this are rarely used at the moment even though they face west and have their own entrance on to the terrace at the side of the house.' He led us through into the bedroom; there was a four-poster bed in it, but my eyes went straight to the double door at the far end —through it I could see into J.B.'s own bedroom.

'It's no good,' said Charles, in a tired whisper. 'She won't share. She couldn't live in

185

somebody else's house, with someone else's furniture, even if you did make this place self-contained.'

'Every woman wants her own kitchen,' I said lightly, trying to lighten Charles' mood.

'Just as long as you realise you're refusing it for him as well as for yourself,' said J.B. He went through into his bedroom and closed the door behind him.

Now he'd made me feel guilty. 'Do you mind, Charles? Is this what you really want?'

'I don't want anything I haven't earned for myself,' he said. I believed him. I kissed him, and he kissed me back, but still his eyes were sombre. Suddenly he started to shiver.

'You're still cold?' I said.

'Reaction—take no notice. I'll be all right after a good night's sleep. I keep thinking of you in that freezer; I ought never to have let you go back into that house. I knew Bianca would hurt you if she could. The worst of it is that I know exactly why I did let you go back; I was the clever one, the one who was going to pull the rabbit out of the hat, and I wanted you to be there to see me do it. I was showing off—and you nearly died because of my selfishness.'

'But I'm all right now,' I soothed him. 'Feel me—I'm warm now and it was only a few minutes . . .'

'It ought never to have happened. I love you and yet I allowed you to be hurt . . .'

He was shivering convulsively now. I pushed him down on to the bed and ran for the door to J.B.'s room. I think he'd been waiting for me to call him, for he was right by the door with a bottle of whisky in one hand and a glass in the other. We got some of it down Charles, and then J.B. said he'd call a doctor.

'No, I'm damned if I'll have any more doctors poking me around,' said Charles weakly. He'd almost stopped shivering, but he still looked terrible.

'You need to get drunk, boy.'

Charles tried to laugh. 'What I need is to get into bed with Sue, and . . .'

'Of course!' said J.B. making for the internal phone. 'I'll have Mrs. Green bring her things up straight away. Better than whisky or the doctor, I shouldn't wonder.'

I didn't argue. I couldn't, with Charles looking at me like an orphan from the storm. My overnight bag appeared within five minutes, by which time I'd got Charles undressed and into bed. J.B. handed me the key of his door, so that I could lock him out, and said he'd make our apologies to the Ashtons.

Charles slept for twelve hours without moving, his left hand wound into my hair so that I couldn't get away, even if I'd wanted to. The next day he got up, but was so far from his usual energetic self that J.B. had the doctor round to check him over. The doctor said he found nothing wrong that a good rest wouldn't cure, and I was driven to work by the chauffeur in the Rolls. I worked the week out and then left. I never did go back to my flat; the yellow carpet fits nicely in my sitting-room downstairs at Whitestones.

We were married very quietly at the end of the week. My parents didn't like the match, but they made the best of it. Perhaps they guessed that making a success of my job at Whitestones would mean that I'd grow away from them. They are proud of me, and uncomfortable in Charles' presence. I don't think he notices.

We didn't have a proper honeymoon. Charles didn't want to go away until he'd seen his father safely back at Green Gables, so we flew to Florence for a few days, and then got back to deal with the alterations at Whitestones and as much of J.B.'s business as Charles wanted to go on handling.

Once I'd accepted that I had to share Charles, I began to like J.B. He is tough, and you do have to stand up to him, but he's a very genuine person, and he loves and needs Charles, as Charles loves and needs him. We did have some rows at first, though. For one thing, J.B. expected me to take over as chatelaine at Whitestones, and act social secretary for him in an unprecedented urge to socialise. I got into a state, Charles told me I didn't have to lift a finger to help J.B. if I didn't want to, and J.B. apologised for trying to browbeat me, and gave me a pearl necklace. So I went to Mary Ashton for advice, and between us we cleared some of the antiques out of the house, found a gardener who didn't mind growing flowers for cutting, and a cook who didn't mind preparing plain dishes as well as doing the fancy stuff on occasion. Gradually Whitestones lost its fusty smell and began to feel more like a house. When I finished the sweater for Charles, I started on another for J.B., but after that it was baby clothes all the way.

Oliver Ashton came home with the first of the spring flowers, a gentle, white-haired, walking skeleton. All his family were there to greet him, including David and Inge with their three little imps. Free of disguise, David was a dapper, brown-haired man with an incisive way of speaking, while I liked Inge at sight for her calm, comfortable manner. I don't think Oliver Ashton ever quite grasped how much Charles had done to obtain his release. I saw them greet each other, and my heart ached for Charles, because Oliver looked at his youngest son as if slightly afraid of him. I even heard him chide Charles for leading Ronald and David into criminal ways, at which Charles bent his head and agreed he'd been much in the wrong.

I cried on the way home. Charles tried to

comfort me, saying he'd always known himself the least loved of his father's sons, and that he'd never expected thanks for what he'd done. J.B. was waiting for us in the hall at Whitestones; before I could stop myself, I flung my arms around him and started crying all over again. Then we had some champagne and got down to making plans for the future.

Jane's baby was still-born, and she has been told it would not be wise for her to have another. I grieve for her and Ronald. When she comes to visit me I put my knitting away and hope my son will not demand too much attention while she is with me. I think Ronald will work her round to the idea of adopting a child one day, but at the moment she won't hear of it. They have stayed on at Green Gables, and the firm of Ashton and Ashton prospers.

Oliver Ashton slipped away from life with the first of the autumn frosts, and all three of his sons wept as they stood by his grave. Mary Ashton did not weep, but lost so much of her previous sharpness of manner that Charles swears she has inherited her husband's meekness of character. I did wonder whether Mary might console herself by marrying J.B., but Charles says she wouldn't be interested, particularly since J.B. is so deeply in love with me. I do wish he wouldn't say such things!

Our first-born came into the world yelling for attention while Charles and J.B. paced up and down the corridor outside, telling each other that there was absolutely nothing to be worried about. Oliver John is nicknamed 'Noll', but he is all Charles to look at, and in character, too. There never was such a greedy, loving little beast. I tell Charles that this next child we're expecting is to be a girl, but I expect he's right, and we'll just go on having boys.

I still see Bessie now and then. She is married and living in the house she picked out for herself long ago, but I don't suppose we shall see much of each other in future, since we are to move to Brussels in six weeks' time. Charles has landed himself a job on some Commission or other there; J.B. is coming, too, and we are to share a big house and employ a ' bonne ' to look after the children. Charles works a twelve hour day, and in his free time has started learning to fly. J.B. proposes to construct a hangar in the paddock and lay out an airstrip beyond, so that we can commute back to Whitestones at weekends.

Outwardly I suppose I've changed; I wear good clothes now, own a big estate car and have an account at three shops in town, and also at Harrods. Occasionally I borrow J.B.'s Rolls and the chauffeur to go shopping, and I've got over being sick with fright before big social functions. Basically I'm still the same. Charles and J.B. knew what they were doing when they latched on to me, for no one else would put up with them. They are a couple of domestic tyrants, throwbacks to the Victorian era. I'm not allowed to wear false eyelashes, or low-cut dresses, or flirt with other men, or even go out for the day without telling them where I'm going. Charles says he doesn't know what I'm grumbling about, as I don't want to do any of those things anyway, but that isn't the point. I agree I don't want to do any of those things, but I ought to be free to do them if I did feel like it.Then he grins and gives me an expensive present, and I tell him he's getting more like J.B. every day.

Nothing about me has really changed. I was born to be a doormat, and that's what I shall be to the end of my days.